THE DESERTED HOUSE

The Deserted House is the story of a middle class woman, Olga Petrovna, a doctor's widow who is left in the early days of the Russian Revolution with a small son to support. She is the sort of woman who makes a respected, loyal citizen in any society; her child is the pivot on which the whole of her life turns. To maintain herself and him, she obtains a post in a Leningrad Publishing House where she gains rapid promotion. Her son becomes a passionately loyal Communist and is selected for an exciting technical post in a distant factory. Quite suddenly the Director of the publishing House is arrested as "an enemy of the people": the great Stalin "Purges" have started. She does not doubt for one moment that he is guilty, and when she hears of other arrests it is with anger and disgust that such apparently worthy people could be guilty of such horrible crimes. When her son, highly praised in *Pravda* only a few weeks before, is himself arrested her immediate reaction is that this is "of course" only an absurd mistake. Then follows the story of her calvary—night after night she has to queue outside the prison and then the Public Prosecutor's office waiting vainly for news that is never given. She still feels that the others in the queue are the relatives of criminals and she herself the only exception, but eventually her eyes begin to open to the truth.

As a documentary of the tragedy, not only of a family but of a whole nation, it is difficult to conceive of a more telling and convincing account of what it meant to "ordinary people". But it is as a work of literature that it should and will be judged by most English-speaking readers. *The Deserted House* is beautifully written with simple economy of language—no "horrors", no physical violence, no scenes of direct cruelty are described, yet the atmosphere is so skilfully conveyed that the reader knows they are taking place. There are neither heroes nor villains, and the author never loses a deft touch of irony and even humour as her characters are brought gently and so vividly to life.

For a long time I had forebodings
of this serene day and the deserted house
The Passage of Time
1939
ANNA AKHMATOVA

LYDIA CHUKOVSKAYA

The Deserted House

TRANSLATED FROM THE RUSSIAN
BY
ALINE B. WERTH

BARRIE AND ROCKLIFF
LONDON

This story was written many years ago, in Leningrad, in the winter of 1939-1940. I tried in this way to record the events recently experienced by my country, my friends and myself. I could not refrain from writing about them though I had, of course, no hope at the time of seeing this story in print. I had little hope, even, that the exercise book, containing the clean copy of it, would escape destruction. To keep it in the drawer of my desk was dangerous; but to burn it was more than I could bring myself to do. I regarded it not so much as a story as a piece of evidence, which it would be dishonourable to destroy.

The war came, and the blockade of Leningrad. The people keeping the manuscript perished, but the manuscript itself survived. I myself left Leningrad a month before the war began, and spent the years 1941-1944 far away from my native city; and it was only at the end of the war that my exercise book, after lengthy peregrinations, found its way back, miraculously, into my hands.

The war ended. Stalin died. My hopes, hitherto unrealizable, that my story could now soon see the light of day, steadily grew.

After the speeches made at the XXth and XXIInd Party congresses, pointing to a better present and denouncing the darker sides of the past, I became more anxious than ever that my story should be made available to readers and so serve to further a cause which I regard as vitally important: in the name of the future, to help to reveal the reasons for and the consequences of the great tragedy my country had suffered.

I do not doubt that literary works describing the Thirties will abound, and that other writers, in possession of far more facts than I myself at that time possessed, besides greater literary gifts and greater powers of analysis, will give a fuller and more complete picture of the life of this period. I have merely tried, to the best of my ability, to record what I personally was able to observe.

But whatever the merits of any future tales or accounts may be, they will all have been written at another period, separated from 1937 by several decades; whereas my story was written with the impressions of events still fresh in my mind. Herein lies the difference between my story and any others which may be devoted to the years 1937-1938. Herein, I consider, lies its claim to the reader's attention.

It is for this reason that I have refrained from making any changes to it, beyond omitting an introductory passage which today seems irrelevant. May it speak today like a voice from the past, the tale of a witness striving conscientiously, against the powerful forces of falsehood, to discern and record the events occurring before his eyes.

The hero of my story, whom I love with all my heart, whom I have tried to re-create in all his beauty, and who was, is and will forever be beautiful is—Truth.

L. N. TOLSTOY

After the death of her husband, Olga Petrovna took a course in typing. She felt she simply had to acquire a profession: it would be some time yet before Kolya began to earn his living. After he got through school, he must whatever happened, sit the exam for admission to an institute—Fyodor Ivanovich would never have allowed his son to go without a higher education.

Olga Petrovna easily got the hang of the typewriter; but then she was much more literate than all these modern young ladies. After getting her certificate, she soon found herself a job in one of the big Leningrad publishing houses.

She became completely absorbed in the office routine, and after a month of it she simply could not understand how she had ever lived without the office. True, it was unpleasant getting up in the cold in the morning by electric light; it was shivering cold waiting for the tram in a crowd of sleepy, scowling people; true, the clatter of the typewriters gave her a headache towards the end of the day. But that didn't matter—it was so interesting being at work! As a child she had loved going to school and used to weep when they kept her at home with a cold, and now she loved going to the office.

Seeing that she was conscientious and discrete, they soon made her senior typist—in charge of the typing pool, so to speak; and it was her job to hand out the work, count the pages and the number of lines, and put the sheets together —and Olga Petrovna liked all this much better than doing the typing herself. Whenever there was a knock on the window, she opened the wooden shutter and took in the papers with quiet dignity. Most of them were accounts, plans, reports, official letters and orders, but now and again there would be a manuscript from some writer.

"It will be ready in twenty-five minutes," Olga Petrovna would say, looking at the clock on the wall, "twenty-five minutes precisely."

And if anyone tried to argue that it was urgent and he had to have it sooner, she wouldn't even listen:

"No, I told you, twenty-five minutes!" and would slam the window to prevent further argument.

She would think a moment, then give the work out to the typist she thought would do that particular job best—if a document was brought along by the secretary of the director, it went to the girl who was fastest, most literate and most accurate.

In her youth there had been days when she was lonely, days when Fyodor Ivanovich—a doctor with a large practice—was away for long periods visiting his patients, and she had dreamed of having her own dressmaking establishment: a large, light room, with pretty girls sitting bent over billowing lengths of silk, and herself showing them the styles and engaging in mundane conversation with elegant ladies when they came to be fitted.

But the typing pool was even better, more serious somehow. Now Olga Petrovna was often the first person to read a new work of Soviet literature, some story or novel, while it was still only in manuscript form; and although she found Soviet stories and novels boring, there was such a lot about battles and tractors and factory workshops and hardly anything about love—she couldn't help being flattered.

She began to wave her hair, which had turned grey early,

and when she washed it, added a little blue to the water to keep it from yellowing. In her simple black overall—relieved by a little collar of real old handmade lace—with a carefully sharpened pencil sticking out of the breast pocket, she felt she looked elegant as well as business-like and efficient.

The typists were a bit afraid of her, and called her the school marm behind her back. But they obeyed her. And she set out to be strict, but just. In the lunch hour, she chatted in a friendly way with those who did their work well and conscientiously, talked about how difficult it was to make out the director's writing and how lipstick didn't suit everyone by any means. But with those who were capable of writing things like "rehersal" or "collictive" she adopted a haughty manner.

There was one typist, Zoya Viktorovna, who really got on Olga Petrovna's nerves. She made a mistake in almost every word, and smoked and chattered impudently all the time she was working. She reminded Olga Petrovna vaguely of a cheeky housemaid they had once had in the old days, whose name was Fanny, and who had been rude to Olga Petrovna and had flirted with Fyodor Ivanovich . . . What's the point of keeping on anyone like that!

Of all the typists in the pool the one Olga Petrovna liked best was Natasha Frolenko, a quiet, rather plain girl with a sallow complexion. She never made any mistakes in her typing, and she always did her margins and paragraphing beautifully. Her work looked as if it was done on special paper and with a better typewriter than the others used. Although in fact both the paper and the typewriter Natasha used were no different from the others, the only difference —just imagine it—lay in her extraordinary efficiency.

The typing pool was separated from the rest of the building by a door in which there was a little window, barred by a small wooden shutter painted brown. The door was always kept locked, and all conversations took place through the window.

At the beginning, Olga Petrovna knew no-one in the place except her own typists and the messenger women who brought along the documents. But gradually she got to know everyone there.

She hadn't been there more than about two weeks before the accountant, a sedate, bald but young-looking man, came up to her in the corridor. He recognized her—some twenty years ago, Fyodor Ivanovich had treated him very successfully when he was ill. The accountant was very keen on boating and Western European dancing, and Olga Petrovna was pleased when he advised her to join their dance club.

The director's secretary, an elderly well-mannered lady, began to say good morning to her; the head of personnel bowed to her; so did a well-known writer, a handsome, grey-haired man who wore a beaver cap and carried a briefcase with his initials on it, and always arrived at the publisher's in his own car.

The writer even asked her one day how she liked the last chapter of his novel. "We literary people noticed long ago that typists are the fairest judges. It's true", he said with a smile, showing his even white false teeth, "they judge a thing spontaneously, without any of the preconceived ideas which affect our friends the critics or editors."

Olga Petrovna also made the acquaintance of the Party organizer, Timofeev, a lame, unshaven sullen fellow, who looked down at the floor when he spoke to you. Olga Petrovna was a little afraid of him. Occasionally he would appear at the window with the assistant manager, and ask for Zoya Viktorovna; then Olga Petrovna would unlock the door and the assistant manager would drag Zoya Viktorovna's machine out of the typing pool into the special department, Zoya Viktorovna following with a triumphant expression. They explained to Olga Petrovna that Zoya Viktorovna had been "security-screened", and the Party organizer summoned her to the special department to type out secret Party documents.

Soon Olga Petrovna knew everyone in the place—their names, their jobs and what they looked like—ledger clerks, editors, technical editors, messengers.

When she had been at the office for a month, she saw the director for the first time. The director's office had a thick carpet on the floor; round the table were deep, soft armchairs, and on the table, three whole telephones, yes three! The director turned out to be a young man, about thirty-five, not more; tallish, well-shaved, wearing an elegant grey suit with three badges, and a fountain pen in his hand. He spoke to Olga Petrovna for two minutes or so, but even during those two minutes the telephone rang three times and as he spoke into one telephone, he lifted the receiver off another. The director himself pushed up a chair for her and enquired politely whether she would be so kind as to stay on late that evening to do some overtime work. She could choose any typist she liked to take down a report from dictation. "I am told that you are very clever at making out my atrocious writing," he said with a smile.

Olga Petrovna went out feeling pride in his power, and flattered by his confidence in her. A nicely-brought up young man. They said that he was an ordinary worker who had made his way—and indeed, he had rather coarse-looking hands—but apart from that . . .

At the first general meeting of the workers of the publishing firm which she attended Olga Petrovna was rather bored. The director made a short speech about the rise to power of the German fascists, and the burning of the Reichstag in Germany, and then drove away in his Ford car. Then came a speech by the Party organizer, comrade Timofeev. He made such long pauses between sentences that you thought he had finished. He was followed by the chairman of the mestkom,* a stout lady wearing a cameo on her bosom who constantly twisted her long fingers while she was speaking. She announced that, in view of what had happened, it was essential to tighten up on working hours and wage a relentless campaign for punctuality. She then went on, in hysterical tones, to make a short statement about Thälmann, and proposed that all workers should join the MOPR.† Olga Petrovna wasn't very clear what it was all about; she was bored, and would have liked to go, but was afraid that wouldn't be the thing to do, and glared at one of the typists who was making her way towards the door.

However, it was not long before even these meetings ceased to bore Olga Petrovna. At one meeting the director, reporting on the fulfilment of the plan, said that the attainment of the high output figures aimed at depended on conscientious, disciplined work by every member of the team—and this applied not to editors and authors only, but also to cleaners and messengers, and to each individual typist. "In this connexion", he said "I would like to say that the work of the typing pool, under the supervision of comrade Lipatova, has already attained an exceptionally high standard."

Olga Petrovna blushed and it was a long time before she dared to raise her eyes again. When she did at last pluck up courage to look round, she thought how kind and nice everyone looked, and even found all the statistics interesting.

* Party or Local Trade Union Committee (T.N.).
† International Aid to Revolutionaries Organization (T.N.).

2

All her free time Olga Petrovna now spent with Natasha Frolenko.

But she had less and less free time. Overtime work or, most often, meetings of the mestkom, of which Olga Petrovna was soon made a member, now took up nearly every evening. Kolya was left more and more often to heat up his dinner himself and he began to call her, teasingly, his "social-minded mother".

The mestkom gave her the job of collecting the union subscriptions. Olga Petrovna gave little thought to the reasons for the existence of the trade union, but it pleased her to rule lines on sheets of paper and mark in the various columns who had paid their subscriptions for the current month and who had not; it pleased her to stick on the stamps and present impeccable accounts to the auditing commission. It pleased her to be in a position to enter the director's imposing office whenever she chose and remind him jokingly that he was four months in arrears and to hear him jokingly present his apologies to the comrades on the mestkom, and watch him pull out his wallet and pay up. Even the sullen Party organizer could safely be reminded that he owed his subscription.

At the end of her first year at the office there occurred an important event in Olga Petrovna's life: she spoke at the general meeting of the workers on behalf of the non-Party employees of the publishing house.

It happened like this. The publishing house was expecting a visit from certain important comrades from Moscow. The assistant manager, a boisterous youth with plastered-down hair, bustled about for days on end, carried round some frames or other on his own back, and sent the floor-polishers into the typing pool just when it was most inconvenient. In the midst of all this commotion, the Party organizer came up to Olga Petrovna in the corridor. "The Party organization, in conjunction with the mestkom" he said, looking as usual down at the floor "is going to ask you . . . to make the pledges on behalf of the non-Party activists."

On the eve of the arrival of the visitors from Moscow there was a mass of work to be done. The pool was kept hard at it typing all sorts of accounts and plans. Practically every evening Olga Petrovna stayed late with Natasha on overtime work. The clatter of the typewriters echoed in the empty room, and the corridors and offices all round were in darkness.

Olga Petrovna liked these evenings. When the work was finished, she and Natasha talked for ages, sitting at their typewriters, before going out into the darkness of the corridor. Natasha didn't say much, but was a wonderful listener. "Have you noticed that Anna Grigorievna" (she was the chairman of the mestkom) "always has dirty nails?", asked Olga Petrovna. "And yet she wears a cameo, and waves her hair. She'd do better to wash her hands cleaner . . . Zoya Viktorovna gets on my nerves terribly. She's so insolent . . . And have you noticed, Natasha, that Anna Grigorievna is always slightly ironical when speaking about the Party organizer? She doesn't much care for him . . ."

After talking about the chairman of the mestkom and the Party organizer, Olga Petrovna told Natasha about Fyodor Ivanovich and how Kolya fell out of his bath when he was six months old, and what a pretty little boy he was, everyone turned round in the street to look at him. He was dressed all in white, a white coat and a white hood . . .

Natasha seemed to have nothing to tell—not a single romance. "Of course, with a complexion like that . . ." Olga Petrovna thought to herself. Natasha had had nothing but unpleasantness in her life. Her father, a colonel, had died in nineteen seventeen of a heart attack—Natasha was barely five at the time. Their house had been taken away from them, and they had to go to live with an aunt who was paralysed. Natasha's mother was a spoiled, helpless woman, they had suffered cruelly from hunger and Natasha had gone out to work when she was not more than fifteen. Now Natasha was completely alone: her mother had died the year before last of tuberculosis, her aunt of old age. Natasha was in sympathy with the Soviet regime, but when she had applied for admission to the Komsomol, she had been turned down.

"My father was a colonel and houseowner and, you see, they don't believe that I can sincerely sympathize with the regime," explained Natasha with a frown. "And perhaps they're right, from the Marxist point of view."

She flushed whenever she talked about being refused admission to the Komsomol, and Olga Petrovna hurriedly changed the subject.

The important day arrived. The portraits of Lenin and Stalin were put into new frames which the assistant manager himself brought along; and the director's desk was covered with red cloth. The Moscow visitors—two stout men in foreign suits, with foreign ties and foreign fountain pens clipped into their breast pockets—were sitting at the table with the director, under the portraits of Lenin and Stalin, and taking documents out of their bulging foreign briefcases. In comparison with them the Party organizer, in his Russian shirt and jacket, looked very insignificant. The boisterous assistant manager and the lift-woman, Marya Karpovna, bustled round, carrying trays with tea, sandwiches and fruit, which they offered first to the visitors and the director and then to all the others.

Olga Petrovna was so excited that she simply couldn't listen to the speeches. As though in a trance, she kept her eyes fixed on the water shimmering in the decanter. At a sign from the chairman, she went up to the table, turned first towards the director and his guests and then to the meeting, and finally stood facing sideways, hands clasped at the waist, as she had been taught to do as a child when reciting greetings in French verse.

"On behalf of the non-Party workers"—she began in a trembling voice, and then went on to pronounce the whole of the pledge to increase the productivity of work, the entire text of the which she and Natasha had composed together and which she had learned off by heart.

When she got home, she didn't go to bed for a long time, but sat up waiting for Kolya, to tell him about the meeting. Kolya was taking his final school examinations and spent every evening at Alik Finkelstein's place—Alik was his best friend, and they were doing their revision together.

Olga Petrovna tidied up the room a bit and then went into the kitchen to light the primus.

There she found the wife of the militia-man, one of the inmates of the flat, a nice, kind woman. She was washing up. "It's an awful pity you don't have a job," she said, "it gives you so many new interests in life. Especially when your work has to do with literature."

At last Kolya appeared, hungry and wet—it was raining outside, the first spring rain; and Olga Petrovna gave him a plate of cabbage soup. She sat down opposite Kolya, her elbows on the table, watching him eat, and was just about to tell him all about the speech she had made when he broke in:

"I've got something to tell you, Mother," he announced proudly, "I am now a Komsomol, the committee approved my application today."

After which he rushed on to tell her about something else, stuffing his mouth full of bread—there had been an awful rumpus at school.

"Pashka Gusev—he's a real old-regime twirp for you . . ."

"Kolya, I don't like you using vulgar expressions like that," Olga Petrovna broke in.

"I know, but that's not the point: Pashka Gusev called Alik Finkelstein a Yid. We decided today at the cell meeting to stage a demonstration trial. And you know who's been appointed as public prosecutor? Me!"

Directly he'd finished eating, Kolya went to bed, and Olga Petrovna, too, went to bed behind the screen; and Kolya, lying there in the dark, recited Mayakovsky to her by heart.

"The man's a genius, isn't he?"

When he had finished Olga Petrovna told him, at last, about the meeting.

"You're marvellous, Mother," Kolya said, and promptly fell asleep.

3

Kolya finished school, the weather turned hot and stuffy, and still Olga Petrovna was given no leave. She had to wait until the end of July. She didn't intend to go away anywhere, but she had been dreaming all through July of how she would be able to sleep as long as she liked in the mornings, and how she would at last be able to do all the odd jobs at home which she hadn't had time for because of the office. She dreamed of getting away from the clatter of the typewriters, of how she would get in the painter to re-paint the door, of going to look for an autumn coat for Kolya and mending his socks; and she simply must go to the cemetery to visit her husband's grave.

But when at last she got her leave, she discovered that after the first day holidays cease to be a pleasure. Olga Petrovna was so accustomed to going to the office that she went on waking up at eight just the same; the painter had finished the door in half an hour; she found a coat for Kolya at once; in two evenings she had mended all the socks; Fyodor Ivanovich's grave was in perfect order ... And the long, empty days dragged by, to the ticking of the clock, occupied only by conversations in the kitchen and with waiting for Kolya to come home for dinner.

Kolya now spent the whole days in the library: he and Alik were studying together for admission to a higher educational establishment, the engineering institute, and Olga Petrovna hardly ever saw him. Occasionally she had a visit from Natasha Frolenko, looking very tired (she was replacing Olga Petrovna at the office); and Olga Petrovna would ask her eagerly about the director's secretary, the quarrel between the chairman of the mestkom and the Party organizer, and Zoya Viktorovna's spelling mistakes. And about the discussion held in the director's office on the novel of that nice writer. The whole of the editorial section had been there . . . "Is it possible that anyone could not like it?", exclaimed Olga Petrovna clasping her hands. "It gives such a beautiful description of pure first love. Exactly like Fyodor Ivanovich and me."

By now Olga Petrovna simply couldn't understand how she had ever lived without having a job. She absolutely agreed with Kolya when he talked about it being essential for women to perform socially useful work. And indeed, everything Kolya said and everything they wrote in the papers now seemed to her to be perfectly natural, just as if people had always talked and written like that.

The only thing Olga Petrovna did regret very much, especially now that Kolya was grown up, was her old flat. Other people had been put into it a long time ago, during the famine years, right at the beginning of the revolution. Fyodor Ivanovich's former consulting room had been taken over by the family of the militia-man, Doroshko, the dining room was occupied by the book-keeper's family, and Olga Petrovna and Kolya were left with Kolya's old nursery. Now Kolya was grown up, and it was essential that he should have a room of his own, after all he was no longer a child . . .

"But, Mother, it wouldn't be right for Doroshko and his children to have to live in the cellar, would it? While we lived in a nice flat? Would that be fair? Would it or not?"— Kolya would ask sternly, and explain to Olga Petrovna the revolutionary significance of the confiscation of bourgeois flats.

And Olga Petrovna was forced to agree with him—it was true it was not quite fair. Only it was unfortunate that the militia-man's wife was such a slut: the sour smell from her room even filtered out into the corridor. She was terrified of opening the window even a crack. Her twins were already over fifteen, but they still made spelling mistakes.

Olga Petrovna had a new title as consolation for the loss of her flat: the tenants elected her unanimously as the official representative of the flat. She thus became, as it were, the boss, the manager of her own flat. She spoke to the book-keeper's wife, gently but persistently, about the trunks standing in the corridor. She worked out how much each person owed for the electricity with the same accuracy as, at the office, she collected the trade union subscriptions. She regularly attended the meetings of official representatives of the different flats organized by the house committee, and then gave the inmates a detailed report of what the house-manager had said.

On the whole, she was on good terms with the inmates of the flat. The militia-man's wife, when she made jam, would always call Olga Petrovna into the kitchen to taste and see whether she had put enough sugar in. And she often came into Olga Petrovna's room, too, to ask Kolya's advice: what could she do to make sure that the twins were not kept down again at school this year—once was enough, heaven knows! And to gossip with Olga Petrovna about the book-keeper's wife, who was a nurse:

"Just try falling into the hands of a nurse like that—she'll have you in the next world before you know where you are!", bluntly declared the militia-man's wife.

The book-keeper himself was already getting on in years; he had flabby cheeks and blue veins were showing on his hands and nose. He was scared of his wife and daughter, and you never heard him in the flat. Not like his daughter, Valya, a ginger-haired girl, who shocked Olga Petrovna by the disrespectful way she talked about her mother: "I'll just show her!", "I don't give a damn!". It was true, of course, that Valya's mother was an awful woman. She would stand by the side of her primus with a stony expression on her face, and keep nagging at the militia-man's wife because her oil stove was smoking, or yell at the twins, who were meek, for not putting the hook on the door when they got in last at night.

She came of the gentry, she used to spray the corridor with eau de cologne, wore trinkets dangling on a chain, and spoke in a soft voice hardly moving her lips, but the words she used were surprisingly coarse.

When pay day came round, Valya would begin to wheedle her mother for money to buy some new shoes with . . . "Get away with you, you cow," her mother would say in her flat voice, and Olga Petrovna, so as not to hear what came next, would hurriedly shut herself up in the bathroom, but it would not be long before Valya came running in to wash her swollen tear-stained face, shouting into the wash-basin all the insults she dared not hurl at her mother.

On the whole, though, flat 46 was a pleasant, peaceful one —not like number 52, above it, where there was positive slaughter almost every pay day. Doroshka, all sleepy after coming off duty, was summoned there regularly, together with the watchman and the house-manager, to draw up a report.

Her leave dragged on and on. She spent it between the kitchen and her own room and when it finally came to an end, Olga Petrovna was very thankful. The wet weather had set in, the Summer Garden was strewn with yellow leaves, trodden into the mud—and Olga Petrovna, in galoshes, umbrella in hand, was again going to the office every day, waiting for the tram in the mornings and, at ten o'clock sharp, with a sigh of relief, hanging her number-card up on the attendance board.

Once again she was surrounded by the thumping and clanging of typewriters, the rustling and crackling of paper, the sound of the window opening and shutting. Solemnly Olga Petrovna handed the director's secretary the carefully sorted pages, clipped together and smelling of carbon-paper; stuck stamps on to the trade union membership cards; sat on the mestkom to deal with the tightening up of discipline at work or the case of some typist or other who had behaved impolitely towards one of the messenger women. Once again she was a bit afraid of the sullen Party organizer, comrade Timofeev; she still disliked the chairman of the mestkom with her dirty nails, secretly adored the director and envied his secretary—but she felt at home with all these people now, they were familiar to her, she felt she belonged there, was not shy any more, and bluntly told off the insolent Zoya Viktorovna. Indeed, why on earth should she be kept on? The matter would have to be raised on the mestkom.

Kolya and Alik passed the examination for admission to the engineering institute. Seeing their names up on the list of successful candidates, they decided to make a radio set in the flat. Olga Petrovna was never very pleased when Kolya and Alik embarked on technical constructions in her room, but she hoped very much that the radio set would cost her less than the ice-boat they'd tried to build not long ago. On finishing school, Kolya had got the idea of building an ice-boat of his own to use on the Gulf of Finland in winter. He got hold of some sort of pamphlet about ice-boats, and procured some planks which he and Alik brought into the room—with the result that it immediately became impossible not only to sweep the floor, but even to get from one part of the room to another. The dining table had to be shoved up against the wall, the divan against the window; there was a huge pile of planks lying on the floor, so that Olga Petrovna was constantly tripping over them. But all her entreaties were in vain. It was useless for her to explain to Kolya and Alik that she couldn't have been more uncomfortable if they had brought an elephant into the flat. They went on planing, measuring, sawing and drawing plans, until such time as they became absolutely convinced that the author of the pamphlet on ice-boats was an ignoramus, and that no ice-boat could ever be constructed from his plans.

Whereupon they simply sawed up the planks and meekly burned them in the stove, together with the pamphlet. And Olga Petrovna put the furniture back in place, and it was quite a week before she got used to the pleasure of having her room clean and unencumbered again.

At first the radio too caused Olga Petrovna nothing but inconvenience; Kolya and Alik crammed the room full of wiring, screws, nuts and bolts and bits of wood; they were up till two every morning discussing the rival merits of various types of receiver; then finally they constructed the receiver, but never let Olga Petrovna listen to anything right through, as they wanted to get something else, Norway perhaps, or England; then they were bitten with a passion for perfection, and spent every evening taking the set apart and putting it together again. Finally, Olga Petrovna took things into her own hands, and then it turned out that wireless was in fact a very pleasant invention. She learned how to switch it on and off herself, forbade Kolya and Alik to touch it and, in the evenings, listened to broadcasts of operas or concerts from the Philharmonic.

Natasha Frolenko also used to come and listen. She brought her embroidery and sat at the table working. She was clever with her hands, she knitted beautifully, sewed, embroidered napkins and collars. The walls of her own room were already covered with things she had embroidered and now she started to embroider a tablecloth for Olga Petrovna.

On her days off Olga Petrovna switched on the wireless first thing in the morning: she liked to hear the weighty, important voice announcing that Perfumery Store No. 4 had received a large consignment of scent and eau de cologne, or that a new operetta was to have its premiere in a few days' time. She simply couldn't prevent herself from taking down every telephone number that was given. The only thing that didn't interest her in the least was the latest news on the international situation. Kolya explained carefully to her all about the German fascists and Mussolini and Chiang Kai-shek—she listened, but only out of politeness. When she sat down on the divan to read the paper, she only looked at the short news items, satirical pieces or the "News from the Courts"; but when she came to the leader or news dispatches, she invariably fell asleep, and the newspaper dropped onto her face. What she liked much better than newspapers were the translations of foreign novels which Natasha took out of the library, things like *The Green Hat*, or *Hearts of Three*.

The eighth of March—Women's Day—was a happy day in Olga Petrovna's life. In the morning the messenger woman from the publishing house brought her a basket of flowers. Amongst the flowers was a card inscribed:

"To Olga Petrovna Lipatova, non-Party worker,
on the occasion of the eighth of March.
From the Party Organization and the Mestkom."

She put the flowers on Kolya's writing table, under the shelf containing Lenin's collected works, and next to the miniature bust of Stalin. All day she felt happy. She decided not to throw the flowers away when they died, but to dry them, and put them away in a book as a souvenir.

4

Olga Petrovna was in her third year at the office. Her pay had been put up, and she now received not two hundred and fifty roubles a month, but three hundred and seventy-five. Kolya and Alik were still students, but they were already earning quite a bit in a drawing office. For Olga Petrovna's birthday, Kolya bought her a little tea service, out of his own money: a teapot, milk-jug, sugar-bowl and three cups and saucers. It was made of thin, good quality porcelain, only Olga Petrovna didn't really like the pattern on it very much—sort of squares, red on yellow. She would have preferred flowers . . . But that didn't matter. It was a present from her son.

Her son had become handsome, grey eyes, black eyebrows, tall, gay and full of calm self-confidence—Fyodor Ivanovich had never been quite like that, even in his best years. Kolya was always clean and smart looking, and cheerful. Olga Petrovna would look at him with tenderness but with a constant undercurrent of anxiety; rejoicing, yet afraid to rejoice. A very good-looking youth, healthy too, he didn't drink and he didn't smoke, was a good son and a loyal komsomol. Of course Alik too was a nicely-behaved young man, and hard working, but nothing like Kolya! His father was a bookbinder at Vinnitsa in the Ukraine, masses of children, living in poverty. Alik, ever since he was quite small, had lived with an aunt in Leningrad, but she obviously didn't look after him very well: the elbows of his jacket were all patched, his shoes were in holes. To look at he was short and puny. And then he hadn't a brain anything like Kolya's.

There was one thing that was a constant worry to Olga Petrovna! Kolya was already over twenty, and he still hadn't a room of his own. She kept on wondering whether her constant presence was not preventing Kolya from leading his own life. Kolya, apparently, had fallen in love with some girl at the institute. She questioned Alik about it, discretely: who was she, what was her name, and how old was she? Was she a good student? What were her parents? But Alik's answers were evasive, and it was clear from the look in his eyes that he was not going to give the secret away. All Olga Petrovna managed to get out of him was the girl's name—Lilya. But it didn't matter what her name was, nor whether it was really serious or just a passing infatuation—the fact remained that it was essential for a young man of his age to have a room to himself.

Olga Petrovna confided her worries in Natasha. Natasha listened without saying a word, then blushed and said that yes, . . . naturally . . . of course . . . it would be better for Nikolai Fyodorovich to have a room of his own . . . but, well . . . she for instance lived by herself with no mother . . . and yet—there was nothing!

Natasha broke off in confusion and fell silent, and Olga Petrovna didn't understand what it was she was trying to say.

Olga Petrovna considered all possible ways whereby she could exchange her one room for two, and even began to put money into her savings bank, so as to be able to pay the extra if necessary.

But the question of a separate room for Kolya suddenly ceased to be urgent: the two best students at the institute, Nikolai Lipatov and Aleksandr Finkelstein, were to be sent as experts under some scheme or other to the Urals Engineering Works in Sverdlovsk. They were short of technicians there. The institute made arrangements for them to complete their studies by correspondence.

"Don't you worry, Mother," Kolya said, putting his great big hand on Olga Petrovna's little one "Don't you worry, Alik and I will manage wonderfully ... We've been promised a room in a hostel ... and Sverdlovsk is not very far away, after all. You'll be able to come and see us some time ... and ... you know what? You can send us parcels."

Every day after that, when she returned from the office, Olga Petrovna spent her time sorting out Kolya's clothes in the cupboard, sewing, mending and ironing his things. She took Fyodor Ivanovich's old suitcase to be repaired. She remembered the spring morning when she and Fyodor Ivanovich went together to buy that suitcase at the Guard Regiment store, but it now appeared to be infinitely remote and unreal, something belonging to a different world. She looked curiously at the page of the *Niva* which had been used to stick up a tear in the side of the suitcase: the lady in the low-necked dress with the long train, and her hair piled up on the top of her head, struck her as strange. That's what the fashions were like in those days.

Kolya's departure worried Olga Petrovna and made her sad, but she couldn't help admiring the skill and care with which he packed his books and the large notebooks filled with his neat writing, and himself sewed his Komsomol membership card into the waist of his trousers.

For a long time the day of his departure was a week ahead—then suddenly it turned out that he was actually leaving the next day.

"Hi, Kolya, are you ready? Kolya!", called Alik, coming

into their room in the morning. His new jacket was rucked up on the shoulders, the corners of his shirt collar crumpled.

Kolya strode over to his suitcase and picked it up as easily as if it had been empty. He carried it all the way to the station without even stopping for breath, whilst poor Alik shuffled along with his little trunk, puffing and blowing and wiping the sweat off his brow with his coat sleeve. With his short legs, and his big head with the protruding ears, he reminded Olga Petrovna of some comic little figure out of a cartoon film. Alik's aunt, of course, couldn't be bothered to go to the station to see him off, so the three of them—Kolya, Olga Petrovna and Alik—walked solemnly up and down the platform in the damp, murky atmosphere of the station.

Kolya and Alik were having a heated discussion about cars: which was stronger and lighter—the Fiat or the Packard? And it was not until five minutes before the train was due to leave that Olga Petrovna remembered she had forgotten either to warn the boys about looking out for thieves on the journey or to give them instructions about their laundry. They must never give things to the laundress without first counting them, and making a list . . . And never on any account eat potato salad in a canteen: it was often left over from the day before—and it was so easy to get typhoid. She took Alik aside and clutched his shoulder:

"Alik, my dear," she entreated, "please look after Kolya for me . . ."

Alik looked at her through his glasses with his big, kind eyes.

"That's no trouble, is it? Of course I'll keep an eye on Nikolai. Of course I will."

It was time to get into the train. A moment later, Kolya and Alik appeared at the window, Kolya tall, Alik no higher than his shoulder. Kolya said something to Olga Petrovna, but she couldn't hear through the glass. He laughed, took off his cap and looked round the compartment, happy and excited. Alik started to tell Olga Petrovna something by writing letters with his fingers in the air. "Don't" . . . she made out, and signed to him, guessing what he wanted to say: "Don't worry" . . . Heavens, they were mere children, and going on such a journey!

A moment later she was walking back along the platform, alone in the crowd, walking faster and faster without noticing where she was going, wiping her eyes with the back of her hand.

5

After Kolya's departure, Olga Petrovna spent even less time at home. There was plenty of overtime work at the office, and she stayed late nearly every evening, saving up money to buy Kolya a suit: a young engineer had to dress decently.

On her free evenings she took Natasha back with her for tea. They would call in at the food store on the corner and choose two pastries, and then Olga Petrovna would make tea in the teapot with the squares on it, and turn on the radio. Natasha brought her embroidery. Just recently, on Olga Petrovna's advice, she had been taking brewer's yeast regularly, but her complexion didn't get any better.

On one such evening, just as she was leaving Olga Petrovna's to go home, Natasha suddenly asked her to give her Kolya's latest photo.

"The only photo I've got in my room at present is my mother's" she explained.

Olga Petrovna gave her the photo of Kolya, handsome and big-eyed, in a collar and tie. The photographer had caught his smile perfectly.

One day, on the way back from the office, they went in to a cinema—and from then onwards the cinema became their favourite form of relaxation. They both loved films about airmen and frontier guards. Olga Petrovna thought the handsome, smiling airmen who performed such great feats, looked like Kolya. She liked the new songs resounding from the screen,—particularly "Warm is my heart" and "When my Country calls me". She liked the expression

"My Country". These words, written with a capital letter, gave her a warm, proud feeling. And when the finest airman or the most courageous frontier guard fell flat on his back, mown down by an enemy bullet—Olga Petrovna clutched Natasha's hand, just as, in her youth, she used to clutch Fyodor Ivanovich's hand, when Vera Kholodnaya suddenly produced a miniature revolver from her wide muff and, raising it slowly, aimed at the vile seducer.

Natasha again applied for admission to the Komsomol, and was again refused. Olga Petrovna deeply sympathized with Natasha's grief: the poor girl was so much in need of company . . . And anyway, why, in fact should she not be admitted? The girl was serious-minded and absolutely loyal to the Soviet regime. For one thing, she worked marvellously, better than any of them. And then, she was politically literate. Not like Olga Petrovna. She never let a day pass without reading *Pravda* from beginning to end. Natasha could talk about everything, just like Kolya and Alik—the international situation, construction under the five-year plan, everything.

And what a state she got into when the "Chelyuskin" was crushed by the ice; she remained glued to the radio. She cut out of the newspapers all the photographs of Captain Voronin, of Schmidt's camp and then of the airmen. When the news of the first rescues was announced, she wept over her typewriter, tears falling onto the paper, and was so overjoyed that she messed up two pages. "They won't let people perish, they won't",—she repeated, wiping her eyes. Such a sincere, warm-hearted girl. And now the Komsomol had turned her down again. It was unjust.

Olga Petrovna even wrote to Kolya about the injustice meted out to Natasha. But Kolya replied that injustice was a class concept, and vigilance was essential. Natasha did

34

after all come of a bourgeois, landowning family. Vile fascist hirelings of the kind that had murdered Comrade Kirov, had still not been eradicated in the whole of the country. Class struggle was still continuing and, therefore, it was essential to exercise the utmost vigilance when admitting people to the Party and the Komsomol. He also wrote that in a few years' time Natasha would, no doubt, be admitted, and strongly advised her to take notes on the works of Lenin, Stalin, Marx and Engels.

"In a few years' time . . ." Natasha smiled bitterly. "Nikolai Fyodorovich forgets that I shall soon be twenty-four."

"Then you'll be admitted straight into the Party," Olga Petrovna told her consolingly. "And what's twenty-four! Its still very young."

Natasha didn't answer but, when she went home that evening, she asked Olga Petrovna for a volume of Kolya's Lenin.

Kolya's letters arrived regularly every week, on Saturday evenings. What a wonderful son he was—never forgot that his mother worried about him, though heaven knows he had plenty to do there! When she got home from work Olga Petrovna started getting her key out of her bag while she was still at the bottom of the stairs, rushed up and, when she finally reached the fourth floor, out of breath, opened the blue post-box. The yellow envelope was already there awaiting her. Sitting down by the window, still in her coat, she took out the carefully folded sheets of Kolya's letter, written on exercise paper.

"Dearest Mother!", every letter began—"I hope you are well, I'm fine. Production at our factory in the past week was . . ."

His letters were long, but mostly about the factory and

the growth of the Stakhanovite movement. About himself and his life—not a word.

"Just imagine"—Kolya wrote in his first letter—"all the worm-gears, milling cutters, even the broaches we have come from abroad, they all have to be bought with gold from the capitalists—we ourselves are still incapable of producing them."

But Olga Petrovna was not interested in milling cutters. What she wanted to know was what he and Alik were getting to eat, whether the laundress there was honest; had they enough money? and when did they have time to study? at night, or what? But Kolya merely skimmed over all these questions, or wrote something incomprehensible. Olga Petrovna so longed to be able to imagine what their room was like, how they lived and what they ate that, on Natasha's advice, she decided to write to Alik.

His answer came a few days later.

"Dear Olga Petrovna!", Alik wrote. "Forgive me for putting it so bluntly, but you're quite wrong to worry about Nikolai's health. We feed quite nicely. I buy sausage in the evenings and fry it in butter for breakfast. We have lunch in the canteen, three courses, not bad at all. The jam you sent we decided to eat only with our tea in the evenings, like that it will last us a long time. I also look after the laundry, and count it. For study, we've put aside a certain time every day. You may be absolutely assured that I do everything I can for Nikolai, as a friend and comrade should."

And the letter ended:
"Nikolai is working successfully on a method for the production of Fellow's cog-wheel cutters in our machine-

tool workshop. The people on the factory Party committee say he's the rising eagle of the future."

Of course, it is the sun that rises, and not eagles, and Olga Petrovna had no idea what a Fellow's cog-wheel cutter was —but all the same, these words filled her heart with pride and admiration.

Olga Petrovna put Kolya's letters carefully away into a box which had once contained writing paper. There too she kept the letters Fyodor Ivanovich had written her when they were engaged, the photographs of Kolya when he was little, and the photograph of the infant Karina, born aboard the "Chelyuskin". Olga Petrovna put Alik's letter there too. She was fond of Alik: he really was devoted to Kolya and understood him very well.

One day, about ten months after Kolya's departure, Olga Petrovna received through the post an impressive looking plywood box. Sent from Sverdlovsk. From Kolya. The box was so heavy that the postman staggered under the weight as he brought it into the room and demanded a rouble "as a tip". "A sewing machine, perhaps?" thought Olga Petrovna. "How marvellous!" She had sold hers when times were hard.

The postman went off. Olga Petrovna took a hammer and knife and opened the box. Inside lay a mysterious black steel object, carefully protected by shavings. Not exactly a wheel, not a bore either. Heaven knows what. Then at last, on the black back of the mysterious object, Olga Petrovna discovered a label, on which was written, in Kolya's writing: "Dear Mother, I'm sending you the first cog-wheel cut with the Fellow's cog-wheel cutter produced in our factory by my method."

Olga Petrovna laughed, patted the cog-wheel and, staggering under the weight, hoisted it on to the window-sill. Every time she looked at it, she felt happy and amused.

A few days after that, when Olga Petrovna was having breakfast, in a hurry to get off to the office, Natasha suddenly burst into her room. Her hair was dishevelled and wet with snow, and one of her boots undone. She handed Olga Petrovna a wet newspaper.

"Just look at this . . . I've just bought it on the corner . . . I was reading it, as usual . . . and there suddenly I see: Nikolai Fyodorovich, Kolya."

There on the front page of *Pravda*, Olga Petrovna saw Kolya's radiant, smiling face. The photograph made him look different, a little older, but there could be no doubt about it, it was Kolya, her son.

Under the portrait was a caption:

"Industrial enthusiast, Komsomol NIKOLAI LIPATOV, who has invented a method for the manufacture of Fellow's cog-wheel cutters at the Urals Engineering Works."

Natasha embraced Olga Petrovna, and kissed her on the cheek.

"Dear Olga Petrovna," she entreated, "please, let's send him a telegram."

Olga Petrovna had never seen Natasha so excited. Her own hands were shaking, too, and she couldn't find her briefcase. They composed the telegram at the office, during the lunch-hour, and sent it off after work. Everyone congratulated Olga Petrovna: at the office even Zoya Viktorovna congratulated her on having a son like that, even the book-keeper's wife.

As she went to bed that evening, happy and tired, it occurred to Olga Petrovna for the first time, that Natasha must be in love with Kolya. How could she not have guessed before! A good girl, nicely brought up, and hard-working—but so very plain, and older than him, too.

Half asleep, Olga Petrovna tried to picture to herself the girl whom Kolya would love, and make his bride: tall, fresh, with pink cheeks and bright eyes and fair hair—like an English print, only with the badge of the K.I.M.* pinned on her breast. Lilya? No, Svetlana would be better. Or Ludmila: Milochka.

* Communist Youth International (T.N.).

6

The New Year was approaching, the year nineteen hundred and thirty-seven. The mestkom decided to arrange a party for the children of the people working at the publishing house. Olga Petrovna was put in charge of organizing it. She took on Natasha as her assistant, and soon the work was in full swing.

They telephoned round to find out the names and ages of the children; typed out the invitations; went round the shops buying sweets and honey-cakes, balloons and crackers, and wore themselves out looking for artificial snow.

The most important and most difficult thing was to choose presents for the children and find something each one would like without exceeding the sum available. About the present for the director's little girl, Olga Petrovna and Natasha almost came to quarrelling. Olga Petrovna wanted to buy her a big doll—bigger than the other little girls were getting—but Natasha thought that would be improper. They compromised on a pretty little trumpet with a fluffy tassel.

At last there was only the tree left to buy. They bought a tall one going right up to the ceiling, with thick branches. On the day of the party Natasha, Olga Petrovna and Marya Karpovna, the lift-woman decorated it, it took them from early in the morning till two in the afternoon. Marya Karpovna amused them with stories about the director's wife; to the director himself she referred, as people used to under the old regime, as "they". She handed Natasha and Olga Petrovna the balloons and crackers, the little post-boxes and silver ships, and they hung them on the tree.

Before long Olga Petrovna's feet began to ache, so she sat down and made up the packets of sweets, with little slips of paper with the words: "Thank you, Comrade Stalin, for a happy childhood."

Natasha finished decorating the tree by herself. She had magic fingers and wonderfully good taste: the way she put up Grandfather Frost was really extremely effective. Then Olga Petrovna stuck the curly head of the child Lenin in the centre of the large red five-pointed star, which Natasha fixed on the very top of the tree—and everything was ready. They removed from the wall the full-length portrait of Stalin and replaced it by another—of Stalin sitting with a little girl on his knee. That was the portrait Olga Petrovna liked best of all.

Three o'clock. Time to go home, rest a little, have dinner and then dress up for the party.

The party was a wonderful success. All the children came, and nearly all the fathers and mothers. The director's wife wasn't there, but the director came and brought his little daughter himself, an enchanting little mite with pretty fair hair.

The children were delighted with their presents, the parents went into raptures over the tree. Only Anna Grigorievna, the chairman of the mestkom, got offended because her son was given a drum and not wooden soldiers like the son of the Party organizer: the soldiers were more expensive. She was wearing a green dress, low-necked even. Her son, a lanky, unpleasant little boy, whistled and ostentatiously broke the drum by banging his fist through it. But all the other children were pleased. The director's little girl was blowing her trumpet all the time, and hopped up and down between her father's knees, pushing her fat little hand against his leg and leaning her head back to look at the tree.

Olga Petrovna felt like the real mistress of the ball. She wound up the gramophone, switched on the radio, showed the lift-woman by a nod of the head, to whom to offer the plates of sweets. She felt sorry for Natasha: the girl was standing timidly against the wall, pale and drab-looking in her best blouse which she had embroidered herself. The director, bending down, took his little girl by both hands and led her up to the tree and warned her Grandfather Frost would gobble her up if she was naughty. Olga Petrovna's heart melted as she watched this scene: she hoped Kolya would be just like the director. Maybe, in a year or two, she too might have a sweet little girl like that, her grand-daughter. Or a grandson. She would persuade Kolya to call her grandson Vladlen*—a lovely name! Or if it was a grand-daughter, Ninel—an elegant, French-sounding name, and if you read it back to front, it became Lenin.

Olga Petrovna, tired out, sank down into a chair. She was thinking it was time she went home, she was beginning to get a migraine, when the impressive-looking accountant approached and, bowing politely, told her a fearful piece of news: a large number of doctors in the city had been arrested. The accountant was personally acquainted with all the leading medical men in the town: no-one could cure his eczema, the late Fyodor Ivanovich was the only one who had succeeded in mastering it. ("There was a real doctor for you! The others sprinkle powders about, smear on ointments, but all to no effect . . .")

Amongst the people arrested, the accountant named

* *Vlad*imir *Len*in (T.N.).

Doctor Kiparisov, a colleague of Fyodor Ivanovich's, Kolya's godfather.

"What? Doctor Kiparisov? . . . It's not possible! But what's happened? Surely not another . . . accident?", asked Olga Petrovna, not daring to pronounce the word "assassination".

The accountant raised his eyes helplessly and went away, walking on tiptoe for some reason.

Two years before, after the murder of Kirov (What grim times those were! Patrols in the streets . . . and when Comrade Stalin was about to arrive—the station square was cordoned off by troops . . . and there were troops lining all the streets as Stalin walked behind the coffin . . .) —after the murder of Kirov there had also been a lot of arrests, but at that time they first picked up all kinds of oppositionists, then old regime people, all kinds of "vons" and barons. But now—it was doctors.

After the murder of Kirov, Madame Nezhentseva was sent away, as a member of the gentry. She was an old friend of Olga Petrovna's, they had even been at school together. At first Olga Petrovna had been surprised: what connection could Madame Nezhentseva have with the murder? She taught French in a school, and lived just like everyone else. But Kolya explained that it was essential to rid Leningrad of unreliable elements. "What exactly is this Madame Nezhentseva of yours, anyway? You remember yourself, Mother, that she didn't recognize Mayakovsky as a poet and used always to say that everything was cheaper in the old days. She is not a proper Soviet citizen." All right, but what about the doctors? what were they guilty of? Just imagine—Boris Ignatich Kiparisov. Such an estimable doctor!

The children were shouting and laughing in the cloakroom. Olga Petrovna, as hostess, helped the parents to find their boots and gaiters. The director, carrying his daughter, came up to say goodbye to her. He thanked the mestkom for the splendid party.

"I saw the portrait of your son in *Pravda*," he told her with a smile. "It's a fine new generation growing up to take our place . . ."

Olga Petrovna looked at him with adoration. She wanted to say that he had no right, yet, to talk about being replaced —what was thirty-five, after all? The prime of life!—but she didn't dare.

He dressed his little girl himself, wrapping her up with a fluffy white scarf over her little fur coat. How skilfully he did everything! Her mother need have no fear about letting him take the child out. A wonderful family man— you could see that at a glance.

7

The papers said nothing about the doctors or about Doctor Kiparisov. Olga Petrovna intended to call in and see Nina Kiparisova, but couldn't bring herself to. There was no time, and anyway it was a bit awkward. She hadn't seen Nina Kiparisova for about three years. She couldn't very well suddenly go and call on her out of the blue.

In January, articles began to appear in the papers about a new trial that was pending. The other trial, of Kamenev and Zinoviev, had made a great impression on Olga Petrovna, but she was too unused to reading the papers to follow it in detail. But now Natasha had got her used to reading the papers, and they read all the articles about the trial together every day. There was more and more talk all over the place about fascist spies, and terrorists, and arrests . . .

Just imagine, these scoundrels wanted to murder our beloved Stalin. It was they, it now appeared, who had murdered Kirov. They caused explosions in the mines and derailed trains. And there was scarcely an establishment in which they hadn't placed their henchmen.

One of the typists in the pool, only just back from a holiday home, related that there was a young engineer who lived in the room next to theirs, she sometimes even went for walks with him in the park. Then one night a car suddenly drove up, and he was arrested: it turned out he was a wrecker. Yet he looked such a decent person—you never could tell!

In Olga Petrovna's house too, in flat 104 opposite hers,

someone was arrested—some communist or other. His room was closed up with red seals on the door. The house-manager told Olga Petrovna about it.

In the evenings, Olga Petrovna put on her glasses—she had recently become long-sighted—and read the paper aloud to Natasha. The tablecloth was already finished, and Natasha was now embroidering a cover for Olga Petrovna's bed.

They discussed how indignant Kolya must be just now. And Kolya was not the only one either: all decent people were indignant. Why, the trains the wreckers derailed might contain children! What utter heartlessness! Monsters! It was not for nothing that the Trotskyists were hand in glove with the Gestapo: they were every bit as bad as the fascists, who were murdering children in Spain. And was it possible that Doctor Kiparisov had taken part in the activities of this bandit gang? He had quite often been summoned for consultation together with Fyodor Ivano-vich. Afterwards Fyodor Ivanovich would bring him home to have a cup of tea. Olga Petrovna could see him in her mind as clearly as she saw Natasha at present. And now he had joined that bandit gang? Who could have thought it? Such a worthy old man.

One evening, after reading in the paper about all the crimes committed by the accused, and hearing the same thing repeated on the radio, she and Natasha had such a vivid picture of heaps of mutilated bodies with the arms and legs torn off that Olga Petrovna was afraid to remain by herself in the room, and Natasha was afraid to walk along the streets. That night Natasha stayed with her and slept on her couch.

Everywhere, in every enterprise and every office, meetings were held, and the publishing house held one too, to discuss the trial. The chairman of the mestkom went round to all the rooms beforehand warning them that in case anyone had so little sense of responsibility as to intend missing the meeting, they would do well to bear in mind that the outside door would be locked. Absolutely everyone came to the meeting, even the members of the editorial section, who usually skipped them.

The director made a speech containing a brief, dry, factual summary of the information given in the papers. He was followed by the Party organizer, Comrade Timofeev. Pausing after every few words, he declared that the enemies of the people were active everywhere, that they might infiltrate even into this establishment and that it was essential, therefore, for all honest workers incessantly to increase their political vigilance. The chairman of the mestkom, Anna Grigorievna, was then called on to speak.

"Comrades!", she began, then dropped her eyes and was silent for a moment. "Comrades!" She clasped her thin hands showing her long nails. "The vile enemy has thrust out his dirty paw to besmirch our publishing house too!"

There was a gasp of dismay. The cameo on Anna Grigorievna's ample bosom rose and fell.

The ex-chief of our printing works, Kuzmin—now unmasked as an enemy of the people—was arrested last night. He turns out to be a nephew of the Moscow Kuzmin who was unmasked a month ago. With the connivance of our Party organization suffering, to use Comrade Stalin's apt expression, from the idiotic disease of complacency, Kuzmin continued, so to speak, to 'operate' in our printing works even after his uncle, the Moscow Kuzmin, had been unmasked."

She sat down, her breast heaving.

"No questions?", asked the director, who was taking the chair at this meeting.

"But what did they . . . do . . . in the printing works?" Natasha asked timidly.

The director nodded at the chairman of the trade union committee.

"What did they do?" she repeated in a shrill voice, rising from her chair. "I think, Comrade Frolenko, I explained clearly enough that the ex-chief of our printing works, Kuzmin, turned out to be the nephew of the other Kuzmin, the Moscow one. He maintained daily contact with his uncle . . . undermined the Stakhanovite movement in the printing works . . . wrecked the plan . . . on the orders of his relative. With the criminal connivance of our Party organization."

Natasha asked nothing more.

Returning home after the meeting, Olga Petrovna sat down to write a letter to Kolya. She told him that in their printing works, enemies had been discovered. How were things at the Ural Engineering Works? Was everything going well there? It was up to Kolya, as a loyal Komsomol, to be on his guard.

At the publishing house, there was a feeling of uneasiness. The director was summoned daily to the Smolny.* The sullen Party organizer kept on coming into the pool—unlocking the door with his own private latchkey—and calling Zoya Viktorovna into the special department. The nice, polite accountant, who somehow always knew everything that was going on, told Olga Petrovna that the Party organization was now meeting every evening.

"There's a bit of a stink," he said with a knowing smile.

* Leningrad Party Headquarters (T.N.).

"Anna Grigorievna is blaming everything onto the Party organizer, and the Party organizer is blaming the director. From what I understand, there's going to be a change of management."

"What are they being accused of?", asked Olga Petrovna.

"Oh, well! they simply can't agree which of them it was that let Kuzmin slip through."

Olga Petrovna couldn't make head or tail of it, and left the office that day with a feeling of vague anxiety.

Going along the street, her eye fell on a tall old woman wearing a scarf over her hat, in felt boots with galoshes on top, picking her way along the slippery pavement with a stick. Her face looked familiar. Why, it was Nina Kiparisova! But surely it couldn't be? Heavens, how she had changed!

"Nina Vassilievna", Olga Petrovna called out to her.

Nina Kiparisovna stopped, raised her large, black eyes and, with an obvious effort, contrived a pleasant smile.

"Good evening, Olga Petrovna! It's ages since I saw you. How's your son? Quite grown-up he must be?" She stood there clasping Olga Petrovna's hand, not looking her in the face, her enormous eyes darting restlessly around.

"Nina Vassilievna", said Olga Petrovna warmly, "I'm so glad I ran into you. I heard that there's been unpleasantness . . . with Boris Ignatich . . . Listen, we're friends after all . . . Boris Ignatich was Kolya's godfather . . . that doesn't count any more of course, but we belong to the old times, you and I. Tell me, is Boris Ignatich being accused of anything serious? Surely there can't be any grounds for such accusations? I simply can't believe it. Such a fine, esteemed doctor! My husband always had the greatest respect for him, and looked up to him as a physician."

"Boris Ignatich did nothing against the Soviet regime," said Nina Kiparisova gruffly.

"I knew it!" exclaimed Olga Petrovna. "I didn't doubt it for a moment, and said so to everyone . . ."

Nina Kiparisova stared at her sombrely with her huge dark eyes.

"Goodbye, Olga Petrovna," she said, without a smile.

"When Boris Ignatich returns, you must invite me round," Olga Petrovna went on. "Why are you so upset about it all? Since Boris Ignatich is not guilty, why, everything will be alright. In our country nothing can happen to a decent and honest person. It's simply a misunderstanding. Don't be downhearted, my dear . . . Come in and have a cup of tea one day!"

She watched Nina Kiparisova walking away along the pavement, tapping the ice with her stick.

"Surely I don't look as old as that?" thought Olga Petrovna. "Her face is all grey and wrinkled. No, its impossible, I don't look like that yet. She's simply let herself go—felt boots, a stick and a scarf . . . It's very important for a woman not to let herself go, to take care of her appearance. Who on earth wears felt boots these days? It's not nineteen eighteen! Why, she looks sixty-five—though she can't be more than fifty . . . It's a relief that Doctor Kiparisov isn't guilty. His wife should know, if anyone does. I always knew it was simply a misunderstanding."

8

The next day, the typing pool was kept busy working on the half-yearly report, which had to be completed urgently. Everyone knew that the director was leaving that night by the "Red Arrow" for Moscow, to report the following day to the Press Department of the Central Committee of the Party on the work of the publishing house. Olga Petrovna urged the typists to hurry. Natasha worked solidly all through the lunch-hour without a break.

By three o'clock the report was already on Olga Petrovna's desk, and she carefully sorted out the four copies, clipping the pages together.

Still the director's secretary didn't come to fetch the report. Olga Petrovna decided to take it along to the director's office herself.

The door was half open; she was stopped on the threshold by the Party organizer.

"You can't go in there!", he said, without even saying good-afternoon to her, and limped away into the other room. He looked all dishevelled.

Olga Petrovna looked through the half-open door. Kneeling in front of the desk was a strange man, pulling papers out of the drawer. Papers were strewn all over the carpet.

"What time will Comrade Zakharov be here today?", Olga Petrovna asked the elderly secretary.

"He's been arrested," the secretary answered in a whisper, "last night." Her lips were blue.

Olga Petrovna took the report back to the pool. As she reached the door, she felt her knees giving way under her. She was deafened by the clatter of the typewriters.

"Do they know already or not?" They sat there typing, as though nothing had happened. If she had been told the director had died she wouldn't have been quite so stunned. She sat down at her desk and began automatically taking off the clips holding the sheets of paper together.

Timofeev came in, opening the door as usual with his own key. Olga Petrovna noticed, for the first time that, for all his lameness, the Party organizer was holding himself erect and walking with a firm step. "Excuse me!" she said, in a scared voice, when he pushed into her accidentally in passing.

Half-past four came at last, and the bell rang. Olga Petrovna went silently downstairs, silently put on her coat and hat and went out into the street. It was thawing. She stopped in front of a puddle wondering how to get round it, when Natasha came up to her. Natasha knew already. Zoya Viktorovna had told her.

"Natasha," Olga Petrovna began, when they came to the corner where they usually parted. "Natasha, do you really believe that Zakharov is guilty? It's nonsense . . . Natasha, we know it is . . ."

She was simply at a loss for words to express her confidence in him. Zakharov, a bolshevik, their director whom they'd seen every day, Zakharov—a wrecker! It was an impossibility, fantastic nonsense, balderdash, as Fyodor Ivanovich used to say. A misunderstanding? But he was such an eminent Party member! They knew him both at the Smolny and in Moscow, he couldn't have been arrested by mistake. He wasn't just anyone, like Doctor Kiparisov!

Natasha said nothing.

"I'll come home with you, I'll explain everything," she said suddenly, and her voice was unusually solemn.

They went in. Took off their coats in silence. Natasha took a carefully-folded newspaper out of her shabby

52

briefcase. She opened out the paper and showed Olga Petrovna a special article on the middle page.

Olga Petrovna put on her spectacles.

"You understand, my dear, he may have been enticed," Natasha whispered, "some woman . . ."

Olga Petrovna began to read.

The article recounted the case of a certain Soviet citizen, A., a loyal Party member, who was sent by the Soviet Government on a mission to Germany to study the application of a new chemical preparation. In Germany, he fulfilled his duties conscientiously until he fell under the spell of a certain S., an elegant young woman who professed to be sympathetic to the Soviet Union. S. paid frequent visits to citizen A. in his flat. Then one fine day A. discovered that certain important political documents were missing from his office. The landlady told him that S. used to come to his room when he was not there; A. had sufficient strength of mind to cut off relations with S. immediately, but not sufficient to tell his colleagues about the disappearance of the documents. He went back to the Soviet Union hoping, by his honest work as a Soviet engineer, to atone for the crime he had committed against his country. For a whole year he worked peacefully, and was beginning to forget about his crime. But the hidden agents of the Gestapo, infiltrating into our country, began to blackmail him. Terrorized by them, A. handed over the secret plans of the factory where he was working. The valiant chekists unmasked the hidden agents of fascism: the trail led back to the unfortunate A.

"You understand?", asked Natasha in a whisper. "The investigation . . . Our director is of course a fine person, a loyal Party member. But citizen A. too, they write here, was a loyal Party member . . . Any

53

loyal Party member can be led astray by a pretty face."

Natasha had no use for pretty women. She recognized only classical beauty, but didn't find anyone who came up to that standard.

"They say that our director did go abroad," Natasha remarked. "Also on a mission. You remember the lift-woman, Marya Karpovna saying that he brought his wife a blue knitted suit from Berlin?"

The article upset Olga Petrovna a great deal, but she still couldn't believe it. This comrade A., whoever he was, was one thing, but their Zakharov was quite another. He was a good Party member; he had himself reported on the trial. Under him, the publishing house had always fulfilled its plan, more than fulfilled it.

"But Natasha, we know . . ." said Olga Petrovna wearily.

"What do we know?" retorted Natasha hotly. "We know that he was the director of our publishing house, and that's all we know, in point of fact. Do you know everything about his life? Can you really vouch for him?"

Well, when you come to think of it . . . Olga Petrovna had not the slightest idea how Comrade Zakharov spent his time when he was not taking the chair at the meetings of the publishing house, or leading his little girl up to the New Year's tree. All men, without exception, were very partial to a pretty face. Any cheeky housemaid could twist any man, even the most decent, round her little finger. If Olga Petrovna hadn't turned Fanny out in time, heaven only knows what her flirting with Fyodor Ivanovich might not have led to.

"Let's have a cup of tea," suggested Olga Petrovna.

Over tea, they remembered that there was something military about Zakharov's bearing. Straight back and broad shoulders. Perhaps he'd been a White officer in his time? He was old enough to have been.

They had nothing to eat with their tea. They were both too tired to be bothered going down to the shop to buy any buns or cakes. "It's going to be grim at the office tomorrow," thought Olga Petrovna. "Like having a corpse in the house. Say what you like, but one's sorry for the director." She remembered the half-open door of his office and the man on his knees in front of the desk. Only now she realized that it was the NKVD conducting a search.

Natasha got ready to leave. She carefully folded the paper and put it away in her briefcase. Then she poured some hot water into her glass and warmed her large, red hands on it before going out. She had got them frostbitten as a child, and they were always chilly.

Suddenly there was a ring at the door, and a second ring. Olga Petrovna went to open the door. Two rings—that was for her. Who could it be, so late?

There on the threshold stood Alik Finkelstein.

Alik there alone, without Kolya—it was unnatural . . .

"Kolya?!" Olga Petrovna grabbed Alik by the dangling end of his scarf. "Typhoid?"

Alik, without looking at her, slowly took off his galoshes. "Shhh!", he said at last. "Let's go into your room."

And he tiptoed along the corridor.

Olga Petrovna, beside herself with anxiety, followed him.

"Don't get frightened, for heaven's sake, Olga Petrovna," he began, when she had closed the door behind her, "calm down, Olga Petrovna, please do. There's nothing to be frightened about. It's nothing terrible. The day before the day before yesterday . . . or when was it? the day before the last day off, anyway , . . Kolya was arrested."

He sat down on the sofa, tore off his scarf, threw it down on the floor and burst out weeping.

9

She must rush off somewhere at once and clear up this monstrous misunderstanding. She must go off immediately to Sverdlovsk and get hold of lawyers and investigators, judges, public prosecutors. Olga Petrovna put on her coat, hat and boots and took the money out of her box. She mustn't forget her passport . . . off to the station at once to buy a ticket!

But Alik, wiping his face with his scarf, said that in his opinion going off to Sverdlovsk at once would be absolutely useless. Since Kolya was a native of Leningrad, who had only recently gone to Sverdlovsk, he'd most probably be brought to Leningrad. Wouldn't she do better to wait a bit before setting off for Sverdlovsk? Supposing she and Kolya missed each other?

Olga Petrovna took off her coat, and threw her passport and money down on the table.

"The keys?! Did you leave the keys there?", she cried suddenly, going up to Alik. "Did you leave the keys with someone?"

"Keys? What keys?" Alik was dumbfounded.

"O lord! how stupid you are!", Olga Petrovna blurted out, then suddenly broke into sobs.

Natasha went up to her and put her arms round her.

"But the keys . . . . of the room . . . in your, what-do-you-call-it . . . your hostel . . ."

They still didn't understand, and looked at her in bewilderment. What fools they were! Olga Petrovna had a lump in her throat, she couldn't get a word out. Natasha poured her out a glass of water.

"But he . . . but he's . . .", sobbed Olga Petrovna, pushing the glass aside, "but he's . . . they must already have let him out . . . seen its the wrong person . . . let him out . . . he's returned home and found you gone . . . and the key gone . . . There'll soon be a telegram from him."

Still in her boots, Olga Petrovna sank down onto her bed. Her head buried in the pillow, she wept and wept, until the pillow was wet through. When she sat up at last, her eyes were sore and she could feel her heart thumping in her breast.

Natasha and Alik were talking softly together by the window.

"Listen," said Alik, his kind eyes looking at her pityingly from behind his glasses. "Natalya Sergeevna and I have decided what to do. Just you go to bed now—you'll have time to go to the prosecutor's office in the morning. Natalya Sergeevna will tell them at the office in the morning that you're ill . . . or make up some story . . . that you got poisoned by fumes in the night . . . any old thing!"

Alik went. Natasha wanted to stay the night there, but Olga Petrovna declared she needed nothing, nothing. So Natasha kissed her and went. She looked as if she'd been weeping too.

Olga Petrovna washed her face in cold water, undressed and lay down. The dark room was lit up from time to time by the sparks from the tram-wires. On the wall and ceiling was a square white patch of light looking like a piece of folded paper. In the book-keeper's room, the nurse was still scolding, while Valya was laughing and squealing.

Olga Petrovna visualized Kolya being taken, under escort, to the official investigator. The investigator—

a handsome soldier, with straps and pockets everywhere.

"Nikolai Fomich Lipatov?", he asked Kolya.

"My name is Nikolai Fyodorovich Lipatov," replied Kolya, with quiet dignity.

Whereupon the interrogator sternly reprimanded the escort and presented his apologies to Kolya.

"Goodness!" he exclaimed. "How didn't I recognize you at once. Why, you are—the young engineer whose portrait I saw recently in *Pravda*! Please forgive me. The point is that a namesake of yours, Nikolai Fomich Lipatov, is a Trotskyist, a fascist hireling and a wrecker."

Olga Petrovna lay awake all night waiting for a telegram. When he got back home to the hostel, and found that Alik had gone off to Leningrad, Kolya would send off a telegram immediately, to reassure his mother. Not until about six in the morning, when the rattling of the trams was starting again, did Olga Petrovna at last fall asleep. She was awakened by a shrill ring which made her heart jump. A telegram for her? But there was no second ring.

Olga Petrovna got dressed, washed and forced herself to drink a cup of tea and tidy up the room a bit. Then she went out into the street in the half-light. It was still thawing, but a thin sheet of ice had formed on the puddles during the night.

After going a few steps, Olga Petrovna stopped short. Where, in fact, had she to go to?

Alik had said to the prosecutor's office. But Olga Petrovna didn't know precisely what the prosecutor's office was, or where it was, either. And the thought of asking a passer-by the way to a place like that filled her with shame. So she went not to the prosecutor's office, but to the prison, as she happened to know that the prison was on Shpalernaya Street.

58

Outside the iron gates there was a sentry standing, with a rifle. The side door next to the main gate was locked. Olga Petrovna tried the door first with her hand, then with her knee, but in vain. There was no sign of any notice anywhere.

The sentry came up to her.

"The gates will be opened at nine," he said.

It was twenty to eight. Olga Petrovna decided not to go home. She walked up and down outside the prison, raising her head and gazing at the iron gratings.

Was it possible that Kolya was there, in that building, behind those iron gratings?

"You are not allowed to walk along here, citizeness," the sentry warned her sternly.

Olga Petrovna crossed over to the other side of the street and walked on mechanically. On her left she saw the wide, snowy expanse of the Neva.

She turned down a street on the left and came out onto the embankment.

Dawn came. It began to get light. On the Liteiny bridge all the lamps went out at once, as though at a word of command. The Neva was piled up with heaps of dirty, yellowish snow. "I suppose the snow from all over the city is dumped here," thought Olga Petrovna.

She noticed a large crowd of women in the middle of the street. Some were leaning against the parapet of the embankment, others walking slowly to and fro, along the pavement or on the road.

Olga Petrovna was surprised to notice that they were all very warmly dressed: muffled in scarves on top of their coats, and nearly all of them in felt boots with galoshes over them. They were stamping their feet and blowing on their hands. "It's obvious they must have been here a long time to have got so cold" thought Olga Petrovna "its not freezing, but thawing again." All these women looked as if they'd been waiting for a train for hours on end at some wayside station.

Olga Petrovna took a careful look at the house, opposite which the crowd of women was assembling—an ordinary house, without any notices on it. What were they waiting for? In the crowd there were both ladies in elegant coats and simple women. For want of anything better to do, Olga Petrovna wandered amongst the crowd. There was one woman there holding one small child in her arms and another, muffled up in a scarf, by the hand. Near the wall of the house there was a man standing alone. All their faces were a greenish colour—or perhaps it was only the half light that made them look like that.

A neatly dressed little old woman with a stick suddenly came up to Olga Petrovna. Under her sealskin cap, pulled low down on her forehead, showed strands of silver hair and dark, semitic eyes.

"Do you want to be put on the list?", she asked kindly. "Number 28."

"What list?"

"L and M . . . Oh, I'm sorry! You were walking up and down here, so I thought you'd also come to enquire about someone who'd been arrested."

"Yes, my son . . . ", said Olga Petrovna in bewilderment.

Turning away from the old woman, upset by her surprising perspicacity, Olga Petrovna went to look for the main entrance of house No. 28. The thought that all these women had come here for the same reason as she had filled her with vague foreboding. But why were they here, on the embankment, and not outside the prison? Ah, yes, outside the prison was the sentry who didn't allow them to wait there.

Number 28 turned out to be an old mansion with the paint peeling off, right near the bridge. Olga Petrovna went into the main vestibule—sumptuous but dirty, with a fireplace, a huge broken mirror and a marble Cupid with one wing missing. On the first step of the majestic staircase lay a woman, curled up on a newspaper, her head propped up on a shabby old briefcase.

"You want to put your name down on the list?" she asked, raising her head. Then sat up and pulled a pencil and a crumpled sheet of paper out of her briefcase.

"I . . . really don't know," said Olga Petrovna distractedly. "I've come to see someone about my son, who was arrested by mistake in Sverdlovsk . . . You understand, they simply mistook him for someone else of the same name."

"Not so loud please," the woman interrupted her angrily. She had an educated, tired face. "Lists are taken away, and then . . . What's the name?"

"Lipatov," Olga Petrovna replied timidly.

"344," the woman said, writing it down. "Your number is 344. Go away, please."

"344," repeated Olga Petrovna, and went out onto the embankment again.

"What's your number?" people kept on asking Olga Petrovna.

Automatically, she kept on repeating it . . .

"You won't get in today then," said a woman, muffled up in a scarf peasant fashion. "We put our names on the list yesterday evening . . ."

"Where's the list?", others went round asking in a whisper.

It was quite light now.

Then suddenly all the people in the crowd began to run.

Olga Petrovna ran behind them. A child muffled up in a scarf burst out screaming. He had bandy little legs and only just managed to keep up with his mother.

The crowd turned down Shpalernaya Street. Olga Petrovna saw in the distance that the little door next to the iron gates was already open. People were squeezing into it like into the door of a tram. Olga Petrovna shoved through also. Then stopped: it was impossible to get any further.

The dark anteroom and the little wooden staircase were swarming with people. The crowd swayed to and fro. People all round were untying their scarves, unbuttoning their collars and elbowing their way about, all looking for the numbers before and after their own. And more and more people kept shoving in from behind. Olga Petrovna found herself being shuttled round. She undid her coat and wiped her face with her handkerchief.

Once she had got her breath and got used to the semi-darkness, Olga Petrovna also began to look for her numbers: 343 and 345. 345 was a man, 343—a hunched ancient old woman.

"Your husband's Latvian too?", the old woman asked, looking up at her with watery eyes.

"No, why?", replied Olga Petrovna in surprise. "Why Latvian? He died a long time ago, but he was Russian."

"I say, have you already got a travel voucher?" someone asked Olga Petrovna. It was the old Jewish woman with the silver hair who had spoken to her on the embankment.

Olga Petrovna made no answer. She simply couldn't understand what was going on here. The woman lying on the stair, and now all sorts of stupid questions about being Latvian, travel vouchers . . . How did travel vouchers come into it? She had the impression that she was not in Leningrad at all, but in some strange, unknown city. She could scarcely believe that only half an hour's walk away there was her office, the publishing house, Natasha typing away . . .

Once they had found the numbers next to theirs, the people stood quietly waiting. Olga Petrovna could see now: the wooden staircase led up to a room which was also filled with people, and it looked as if there was another room beyond that.

She began furtively to examine the people round her. That woman with the briefcase, with the woollen socks pulled on over her stockings and clumsy shoes—she was the one who had been lying on the stair. Here too people kept on coming up and speaking to her, but she wasn't taking down names any longer: it was too late.

To think that all these women were the mothers, wives and sisters of wreckers, terrorists and spies. And the man— the husband or brother of one! They looked like perfectly ordinary people, just like those you see in trams or shops. Except that they all looked tired and baggy-eyed. "I can imagine how terrible it must be for a mother to learn that her son is a wrecker," thought Olga Petrovna.

Now and again a woman would come down the narrow, creaking staircase, elbowing her way with difficulty through the crowd.

"Did they accept it?" people asked her when she got to the bottom.

"Yes, yes!", and she showed them a pink slip.

But one of them—a milk-woman, by the look of it, she was carrying a large milk-can—replied: "Deported!"— and, putting down her can, burst into loud sobbing, leaning her head against the doorpost. Her kerchief slipped down, showing her reddish hair and pretty little earrings.

"Quiet!" people shushed at her from all sides. "He

doesn't like it when there's a noise, he'll shut the window and that will be the end of that. Quiet!"

The milk-woman straightened her kerchief and went out, tears rolling down her cheeks.

Olga Petrovna realized from what she heard people saying that most of these women had come to hand in money for husbands and sons who had been arrested—or else to find out whether they were here. Olga Petrovna felt her head beginning to swim from stuffiness and tiredness. She was terrified that the mysterious little window they were all pushing towards would be shut before she got there.

"If it closes at two today, we shan't get there," the man said to her.

"At two? Surely I don't have to stay here till two?", thought Olga Petrovna miserably. "It can't be more than ten yet!"

She closed her eyes, to try to stop her head swimming. There was a constant buzz of scraps of whispered conversation:

"When was your's picked up?"

"More than two months ago."

"Two weeks ago—mine."

"I say, you don't know where else you can make enquiries?"

"At the prosecutor's office. But they don't tell you anything anywhere."

"Have you been to Chaikovsky Street? And Herzen Street?"

"Herzen Street is for the military."

"When was your's picked up?"

"It's my daughter."

"At Arsenal Street, apparently, they accept clothes."

"You're what, Latvians?"

"No, we're Poles."

"When was your's picked up?"

"It's six months already."

"What number have we reached?"

"Twenty something."

"Not more? Heavens above! Let's only hope he doesn't close at two! Last time he slammed down the window at two sharp!"

Olga Petrovna rehearsed to herself what she was going to ask: "Had Kolya been brought to Leningrad? When was it possible to see the judge—or, what was he called, the investigator? Couldn't she see him today? And couldn't she have an interview with Kolya immediately?"

In two hours Olga Petrovna, behind the old woman, reached the first step of the wooden staircase. In three hours, she reached the first room. In four hours, she was in the second room and in five—following the winding queue—she was back in the first room again. She could make out the little wooden-framed window and, through the window the broad shoulders and big hands of the burly official. It was three o'clock. Olga Petrovna counted up: there were fifty-nine people in front of her.

Each woman, when her turn came, gave the name and timidly handed the money in at the window. The bandy-legged little boy was sobbing and licking his tears away with his tongue. "Just wait, I'll talk to him," thought Olga impatiently. "He'd better just take me at once to see the investigator, the prosecutor . . . or whoever it is . . . How uncivilized things still are with us in some ways! Such a fug, they can't even ventilate the place. Someone ought to write a letter to *Leningrad Pravda* about it."

At last there were only three people left in front of Olga

Petrovna. She also got some money ready, just in case. Kolya mustn't be short, meantime.

The bent old woman with a trembling hand handed in thirty roubles at the window, and received in return a pink receipt, at which she peered short-sightedly.

Olga Petrovna quickly took the old woman's place. Behind the window she saw a burly young man with a puffy white face and sleepy little eyes.

"I would like to know," began Olga Petrovna, bending the better to see the face of the man behind the window "if my son is here? The point is that he was arrested by mistake . . ."

"Name," the man interrupted.

"Lipatov. He was arrested by mistake, and it's several days now since . . ."

"Just a moment, citizeness," said the man, leaning over a drawer containing cards. "Lipatov or Lepatov?"

"Lipatov. I would like to go at once to see the prosecutor or anyone you care to direct me to . . ."

"Letters?"

Olga Petrovna didn't understand.

"First name?"

"Ah, initials? N.F."

"N or M?"

"N, Nikolai."

"Lipatov, Nikolai Fyodorovich," the man read out, taking a card out of the drawer: "He's here."

"I would like to know . . ."

"We give no information. That's all, citizeness. Next!"

Olga Petrovna hastily pushed the thirty roubles through the window.

"He's not allowed money," the man said, pushing the money aside. "Next! Move on, please, don't get in the way."

"Go on!", people whispered to Olga Petrovna from behind. "Otherwise he'll slam down the window."

It was getting on for six when Olga Petrovna reached home. She found Alik and Natasha in her room. She sank down on a chair and it was some minutes before she summoned the strength to take off her outdoor things. Alik and Natasha looked at her questioningly. Then she told them that Kolya was here, in prison, on Shpalernaya Street, but simply couldn't explain to them how it was she hadn't found out the reason for his arrest, or when she would be allowed to go and see him.

10

Olga Petrovna took two weeks' leave without pay from the office. While Kolya was in prison, she simply couldn't think about all sorts of papers, or about Zoya Viktorovna. In any case, there wasn't time to go to the office: she had to stand in queues day and night.

She sent in her application to the lame Party organizer: after the arrest of Zakharov, he had been appointed, temporarily, acting director. He now sat in the office where Zakharov used to sit, behind the same large table with the telephones. He no longer wore a Russian shirt, but a grey suit from the Leningrad Clothing Stores, with collar and tie—but he still looked insignificant.

Olga Petrovna explained that she needed the leave for domestic reasons. Timofeev slowly wrote out a certificate in red ink. Without looking at Olga Petrovna, he then stated that she would be replaced this time by Zoya Viktorovna, to whom she should hand over.

"Why not Frolenko?", Olga Petrovna asked in surprise. "Zoya Viktorovna is not properly literate, and makes mistakes in spelling . . ."

Comrade Timofeev made no reply, and stood up.

Oh! What did it matter? Olga Petrovna left the room. She had to hurry to go and queue up.

All her days and nights now were spent neither at home nor at the office, but in a strange new world—the world of queues. Sometimes on the embankment of the Neva, sometimes on Chaikovsky Street—there were benches there, you could sit down—sometimes in the enormous hall of the Big House, sometimes on the staircase in the prosecutor's office. She only went home to eat or have a sleep when Natasha or Alik kept her place in the queue. (The director had given Alik permission to go to Leningrad for one week only, but he kept on putting off his return to Sverdlovsk in the hope that he and Kolya would be able to return together.)

Olga Petrovna had learned a lot of things during those two weeks: she had learned that you must go at night to put your name down on the list, at about eleven or midnight, and appear every two hours for the roll-call, though it was better not to go away at all, as they might strike you off the list; that you simply must take a warm scarf and put on felt boots—otherwise, even when it was thawing, you'd be shivering with cold between three and six in the morning, and your feet would be freezing; she learned that the lists were taken away by NKVD officials, and those who made out the lists were taken off to the militia; that you must go to the prosecutor's office on the first day of the week, and there they received everyone, and not in alphabetical order—whereas on Shpalernaya Street the days for "L" were on the 7th and the 20th (the first time she chanced, miraculously, to go on the right day); that the families of those who had been arrested were sent away from Leningrad—you got a "travel voucher" not for a sanatorium, but for deportation; that on Chaikovsky Street information was given out by a red-faced old man with a bushy moustache like a cat's, at the prosecutor's office by a young lady with a peaky nose and crinkly waved hair; that on Chaikovsky Street you had to show your passport, on Shpalernaya Street —not; she learned that, amongst the enemies unmasked, there were a lot of Latvians and Poles—that explained why there were such a lot of Latvian and Polish women in the queues. She was soon able to pick out at a glance which of the people in Chaikovsky Street were not casual passers-by but going to queue up, even in the tram she could see from their eyes which of the women were on their way to the iron gates of the prison. She became familiar with all the main and back staircases in the buildings along the embankment and could always find the woman with the list wherever she happened to conceal herself. She knew now, when she left home after a short sleep, that wherever she went—on the street, on the staircases, in the corridors, the hall in Chaikovsky Street, the embankment, the prosecutor's office—she would always find women, women and more women, old and young, in kerchiefs or in hats, alone or with children or babes in arms, children crying from lack of sleep, and frightened, silent women; and as in her childhood, after an excursion to the forest, when she screwed up her eyes she saw nothing but berries, berries and more berries—so now, whenever she closed her eyes, she saw faces, faces, and more faces . . .

But there was one thing she did not find out in the course of these two weeks: what had Kolya been arrested for? and who was going to try him, and when? and what was he accused of? and when would this stupid misunderstanding finally be cleared up, and when would he return home?

At the information office on Chaikovsky Street, the red-faced old man with the bushy moustache looked at her passport and asked: "What is your son's name? You're his mother? Why doesn't his wife come? Not married? Lipatov, Nikolai? Being investigated," and thrust her passport back through the window; and before Olga Petrovna had time to open her mouth, the automatic shutter dropped down with a bang and there was a ring, meaning: "Next!" There was no point in talking to the shutter,

70

so Olga Petrovna after waiting a moment, went away.

At the prosecutor's office, the peaky-nosed young lady with the crinkly hair stuck her head out of the window and rapped out: "Lipatov? Nikolai Fyodorovich? Not yet reached the prosecutor's office. Enquire again in two weeks."

On Shpalernaya Street, the burly, sleepy official invariably pushed aside her money, with the words: "He's not allowed it." That was all she knew about Kolya! Others were allowed money but he, for some reason, was not. Why? But she understood already that to question the person behind the window was utterly useless.

On the other hand she questioned Alik avidly about what had happened when they took Kolya away.

And Alik patiently recounted, again and again, how they had been already asleep, when suddenly there was a knock at the door and the manager of the hostel came in, followed by the superintendent and behind him, someone in civilian clothes and another person in military uniform.

"What time was it?", Olga Petrovna asked.

"Oh, about half-past one or so," replied Alik and went on: "The superintendent turned on the light, and the civilian asked: 'Which of you is Lipatov, Nikolai?'"

"Kolya was scared?", Olga Petrovna broke in nervously.

"Not in the slightest," replied Alik. "He got dressed quickly and asked me to tell them at the factory next day that he'd been arrested by mistake, and that he might be away for several days ... Let Motya Roitman take his place at the factory—that's a Komsomol who works there ..."

"And is it true he took nothing with him, absolutely nothing?" Olga Petrovna anxiously clasped her hands.

Alik explained that Kolya absolutely refused to take either a change of linen or a towel, although the washer-woman had just brought the things back. "What for? I shall be back tomorrow or the day after."—"I strongly advise you to take them," said the officer pointedly. But Kolya told him too that there was no point: he'd be back the next day.

"That just shows what a clear conscience he had!" Olga Petrovna was deeply moved. "Will they give him a towel there do you think?"

Alik had waited patiently for Kolya to return one day, two, three ... it was not until the fourth day that he decided to go off to Leningrad—to get the matter cleared up. He told the director a tale about his mother being on the point of death. And the director—a good-hearted fellow—gave him permission to go.

Olga Petrovna questioned Alik closely: perhaps Kolya had quarrelled with the bosses? Been rude to someone? Gone round with someone who later turned out to be a wrecker? Or some woman, perhaps, had led him astray?

"Some woman indeed, what next?", Alik was a bit annoyed. "And anyway, can you imagine Nikolai being led astray? Surely you know him better than that? Our director said quite openly about him that he'll be a world-famous engineer."

Yes of course, of course, Kolya was simply not capable of doing anything wrong. She, Olga Petrovna, should know what a heart of gold he had, and what a brain, and how absolutely loyal he was to the Soviet regime and the Party. But at the same time there was a reason for everything. Kolya was still very young, and he had never been left on his own. He must have put someone's back up. You had to learn how to get on with people.

And Olga Petrovna looked at Alik with a touch of hostility: he hadn't kept an eye on Kolya properly. If only Kolya had remained in Leningrad, under his mother's eye, nothing would have happened to him. She should never have let him go off to Sverdlovsk.

But even so, even so, nothing terrible could happen, Olga Petrovna went on persuading herself. She expected Kolya to arrive home any moment. Whenever she went off to queue up, she left the key to her room on the shelf in the corridor, in the usual place. She even left hot soup ready for him in the oven. And each time she came back, she hurried upstairs without pausing for breath, as she used to on the days when she was expecting his letters: she'd go into the room and find Kolya there waiting for her, wondering where on earth his mother had got to.

There had been a woman in the queue, last night who had said—Olga Petrovna heard her: "Come back! That's what you think! Anyone who gets in here doesn't come back!" Olga Petrovna wanted to stop her, but what was the good. In our country innocent people don't disappear. Particularly Soviet patriots, like Kolya. They'll clear the matter up and let him out.

One evening Alik persuaded Olga Petrovna to lie down for an hour or so, then put on his coat and scarf and left: it was the 19th—he was going to queue up in Shpalernaya Street.

"I'll be there by two," called Olga Petrovna from her bed, in a weak voice.

"Olga Petrovna, five will be quite time enough," he answered cheerfully, and went out of the door.

Then for some reason he came back again. He went up to Natasha, who was sitting beside the window, knitting.

"What do you think, Natalya Sergeevna," he asked, his bright eyes, from behind the glasses, looking her straight in the face, "all those people in prison, are they no more guilty than Kolya is? All those mothers standing in queues somehow look awfully much like Olga Petrovna."

"I don't know." Natasha had become very uncommunicative, lately.

She had never been talkative, but ever since Kolya had been arrested, she scarcely spoke at all. In answer to questions she replied only: "yes," "no," or "I don't know." Even if she'd been asked what her own name was, she'd probably only have said "I don't know." When not at the office she spent all her time with Olga Petrovna—cooking the dinner, washing the dishes, giving her water with valerian drops—or else standing in queues. And all the time, she never opened her mouth.

"But, Alik," Olga Petrovna said quietly, "how can you even compare them? Kolya was arrested by mistake, whereas the others . . . Don't you read the papers, or what?"

"Uh! the papers . . ." said Alik, going out.

The papers were beginning to publish the confessions made by the accused at their trial. In the queue the day before, Olga Petrovna had read a whole page over the shoulder of the man standing in front of her. Her legs were aching and her heart was heavy, but the paper was so interesting that she craned her neck and read the whole thing through. The accused gave all the details about the murders and poisonings and explosions—and Olga Petrovna shared the prosecutor's indignation. "What do we call such things?" the prosecutor asked the accused with controlled anger. "Vile treachery!", the accused replied contritely.

No, Olga Petrovna had been quite right to keep aloof from her neighbours in the queue. She was sorry for them, of course, as human beings, for the children in particular; but still an honest person must remember that all those women were the wives and mothers of poisoners and spies and murderers.

74

11

Two weeks passed. Alik returned to Sverdlovsk, to the works; Olga Petrovna went back to work at the publishing house—still having found out nothing about Kolya.

The women in the queue explained to her that the case would doubtless reach the prosecutor's office, eventually, and when that happened, she would be allowed to go and see the prosecutor. He received people not through a hatch but behind a table and you could tell him everything.

For the moment there was only one thing for it—to go to the office, count the lines, smile, hand out the work and, to the bang and clatter of the typewriters, go on thinking of Kolya every moment. Kolya sitting in prison, Kolya—in prison! Along with bandits and spies and murderers. In a cell. Locked up.

Whenever she tried to visualize the cell, and Kolya in it, she invariably thought of the picture of Princess Tarakanova; a girl with dishevelled hair cowering against a black wall, water flooding the cell, rats . . . but in Soviet cells, of course, it was not like that.

Alik, when he said goodbye, advised her not to tell anyone about Kolya being arrested.

"I've no reason to be ashamed of Kolya . . .", she was about to get angry, but then agreed Alik was right: other people, after all, didn't know Kolya, and heaven only knows what they might not imagine.

So she told no-one, either at the office or in the flat—only the militia-man's wife, who found her one day weeping in the bathroom. The militia-man's wife sighed sympathetically: "It's no use weeping—he may still return," she said consolingly. "I've noticed you, running round day and night, you're looking like death."

Five months had passed since the day of Kolya's arrest—winter had been followed by spring, spring by the stifling heat of June—and still no sign of Kolya. Olga Petrovna was worn out with the heat and the waiting.

Five months, three weeks and four days . . . and five days . . . and six days.

Five months and four weeks . . . And Kolya had still not returned home, money was still not allowed him, and Olga Petrovna suddenly began to have unpleasantnesses at the office. One thing after another.

The person responsible for the unpleasantness was Zoya Viktorovna.

When Olga Petrovna returned to the office after her two weeks' leave, Zoya Viktorovna had been appointed as her assistant: she had to check the typed pages. Olga Petrovna knew that she was no help at all: she was illiterate herself! How could she correct other people's mistakes? . . . But there was no going against Timofeev's decision. So Zoya Viktorovna did the checking, and Olga Petrovna said nothing.

Then one day Comrade Timofeev, rattling with keys—he now carried round with him all the keys to all the desks and all the rooms—stopped Olga Petrovna in the corridor and asked her to send Natasha to his office after work. Olga Petrovna sent Natasha to him, and waited for her in the cloakroom, wondering what on earth Comrade Timofeev could want with Natasha.

Natasha came back fairly soon. Her pale face was impassive, only her lips were trembling slightly.

"I've been dismissed," she said, when they got out into the street.

Olga Petrovna stopped short.

"Zoya Viktorovna showed the Party organizer the piece I typed yesterday. You remember, the long article about the Red Army? I had written in one place R*a*d Army, instead of R*e*d."

"But for heaven's sake," Olga Petrovna expostulated, "that's just a typing mistake. Why imagine you'll be dismissed tomorrow? Everyone knows you're the best typist in the pool."

"He said: you will be dismissed for lack of vigilance."

Natasha walked straight ahead. The sun was shining right into her face, but she didn't even lower her eyes.

Olga Petrovna took her home with her, and gave her tea. There was no Kolya. Before, when Kolya had been living happily in Sverdlovsk, Olga Petrovna hadn't been miserable because he wasn't with her; only a bit lonely. Now every object in the room seemed to be wailing to Olga Petrovna that Kolya was gone. On the windowsill, all alone, stood the black cog-wheel.

"I'll go to the office tomorrow, but it will be the last time," said Natasha, as she went away.

"Don't talk nonsense!" Olga Petrovna called after her. "That can't happen."

But it seemed that it could. There appeared on the notice-board, the next day, the announcement of the dismissal of N. Frolenko and E. Gorskaya—the former secretary of the director. The reason given for the dismissal of Frolenko was lack of political vigilance, for that of the secretary—association with an enemy of the people, the former director Zakharov.

Next to this announcement was a large notice:

A GENERAL MEETING
5 P.M. TODAY
FOR ALL STAFF MEMBERS
AGENDA:

1. Report by Comrade Timofeev on wrecking activities on the publishing front.
2. Other business.

ATTENDANCE COMPULSORY

Natasha took her briefcase and went off as soon as the bell rang, saying to everyone: "Goodbye!"—"Good luck!" replied the typists in unison; only Zoya Viktorovna said nothing: she was busy doing her hair, looking at her reflexion in the window pane.

Olga Petrovna, with a heavy heart, accompanied Natasha as far as the cloakroom: "Come this evening," she whispered as she said goodbye.

The chairman of the mestkom was already summoning everyone to the director's office. The lift-woman, Marya Karpovna, was bringing in the chairs. Olga Petrovna went in and sat down in the front row. She felt frightened and alone. The centre light was lit and the heavy curtains drawn. The staff were coming in and taking their places. All their faces betrayed a kind of eager, anxious curiosity.

"Well, comrades, do we have to send you a special invitation?" cried the chairman of the mestkom, going into the editorial department.

Timofeev was standing at the table turning over the papers.

The chairman of the mestkom declared the meeting open. She was unanimously elected, by a half-hearted show of hands, to preside over it. Comrade Timofeev cleared his throat.

"Comrades! we are meeting today to discuss an important matter," he began, "to take n-note of a criminal lack of vigilance in our publishing house, and consider how to liquidate the consequences." For once he spoke smoothly and with confidence, almost without stammering. "For five whole years, under our very noses, so to speak, there operated in our community an individual now exposed as an enemy of the people, an evil bandit, a terrorist and a wrecker—ex-director Zakharov. Zakharov has no longer power to wreck. But in his time he brought along with him a whole train of his puppets, his retinue, if I may put it like that, who helped him build up a strong nest in our midst, and assisted him in all kinds of ways in the pursuit of his filthy trotskyist machinations. To the shame of our community, Zahkarov's retinue has still not been liquidated. I have here in front of me,"—he turned over the papers— "I have here certain documentary data which give you documentary proof of their filthy counter-revolutionary activities."

Timofeev paused and poured himself out some water.

"What do these documents show?" he continued, wiping his mouth with the palm of his hand. "This document here contains irrefutable proof that, in the year nineteen hundred and thirty-two, on the personal initiative of the director, without reference to the mestkom and the personnel department—I repeat, on the personal initiative of the director, a certain N. Frolenko was appointed on the staff."

Olga Petrovna shrank back, as though her own name had been mentioned.

"And who is this Frolenko? She is—the daughter of a colonel, the proprietor, under the old regime, of a so-called estate. What, you may ask, was citizeness Frolenko doing in our midst, the daughter of an alien element, appointed by the bandit Zakharov? The answer to this question is provided by another document. Under the wing of Zakharov, citizeness Frolenko learned to blacken our beloved Red Army of Workers and Peasants, to strike counter-revolutionary blows: she called the Red Army—the Rat Army."

Olga Petrovna felt her mouth go dry.

"And the ex-secretary Gorskaya? She was the director's loyal accomplice, the person on whom he could rely implicitly in all his so-called activity. How did it come about that this wrecker and his retinue were able, for five whole years, to bamboozle Soviet society? This, comrades, can be explained by one thing only: the criminal relaxation of political vigilance."

Comrade Timofeev sat down and took a drink of water. Olga Petrovna looked thirstily at the water: her mouth and throat were feeling completely parched.

The chairman of the mestkom rang the bell sharply, though no-one had moved or uttered a word.

"Does anyone wish to make any comments?" she asked.

Silence.

"Comrades, does anyone wish to speak?" the chairman asked again.

Silence.

"Is there really no-one who wishes to comment on this vitally important topic?"

Silence. Then suddenly, from the door, came a loud voice. All heads turned to look.

It was the lift-woman, Marya Karpovna. Up till now, she had never spoken at any meeting. Indeed, few people in the place had ever heard her voice.

"Please, please, this way, comrade Medvedeva!"

And the lift-woman trundled up to the table.

"I 'ave me proletarian say in this too. For that secretary, it's quite right, citizens. Get into the lift in 'er giloshes she would, leave 'er dirty foot-marks all over the show—and you go and wipe up after 'er. 'Er making the mess, and me wiping up. Take 'er up in the lift yer do, then she shoves in and makes yer take 'er down again. Up 'undred times, and down agin. Yer can't refuse, with 'er shoving in with the director all the time, following 'im around she was. 'E comes into the lift, and there she'll be after him, 'e gets into the car, and there she'll be sitting beside 'im. Course they worked 'and in glove. But I want to tell comrade Timofeev —in plain, proletarian language—'ow many times I sed to 'im: just send 'er packing, I sed, 'er 'nd 'er lardy-da airs! But 'e dont give a damn 'e don't, just sez nothing and goes off. What do yer think, Comrade Timofeev, a lift-woman's just nobody, don't understand nothing? Yer make a mistake! This aint the old days any more! Under the Soviets there aint no nobodies—we're all somebody now!"

"Quite true, Comrade Medvedeva, quite true," said Anna Grigorievna. "Does anyone else want to speak?"

Silence.

"May I say a word?" asked Olga Petrovna quietly. She stood up, then sat down again. "I only want to say a few words, about Frolenko ... Of course, it was a dreadful thing she wrote, dreadful. But everyone can make mistakes, can't he? She wrote not Red, but Rad simply because, on the typewriter—as every typist knows—the letter *a* is near the letter *e*. Comrade Timofeev said she wrote Rat, but she didn't, she wrote Rad, which is not at all the same thing ... there's nothing bad about it. It was simply a typing error. Frolenko is a highly qualified typist, and very conscientious. It was pure chance that she made such a mistake."

Olga Petrovna fell silent.

"Are you going to reply?", said the chairman of the mestkom turning to Timofeev.

"Documents" . . . declared Timofeev rapping the papers with his knuckles. "There's no getting over documents, Comrade Lipatova. Rad or Rat—its all the same. A clear case of an act of class hostility on the part of citizeness Frolenko."

"Does no-one else wish to speak? . . . I declare the meeting closed."

The people dispersed quickly, in a hurry to get home. From the cloakroom came a buzz of conversation: about No. 5 trams being few and far between, about the children's department in the Arcade getting in a consignment of excellent gaiters. The accountant invited Zoya Viktorovna to go boating with him.

"You and your boating!" she scoffed, pouting her lips at the mirror as though to be kissed. "To go to the cinema wouldn't be bad!"

About the meeting, or wrecking activities—not a word!

Olga Petrovna went quickly home, without even noticing where she was going. She had an idea that when she got into her room and closed the door, her head would cease aching, all this would stop, and she would feel alright. Her temples were throbbing. Why was her head aching so? People hadn't been smoking at the meeting. Poor Natasha! She really had no luck! A first-class typist, and suddenly . . .

There was a note waiting for her at home:

"Dear Olga Petrovna! I've come back again. Motya Roitman reported me to the Komsomol, saying that I had been associated with Nikolai. I have been expelled from the Komsomol thanks to the fact that I refused to dissociate myself from Nikolai, and dismissed from work. It is hard to be excluded from the ranks. I'll pop in tomorrow. See you soon! Your Aleksandr Finkelstein."

Olga Petrovna stood looking at the note. Heavens, so much unpleasantness everywhere, all at once! First Kolya, then Natasha and now Alik.

But Alik, no doubt, was at fault himself: he must have said something silly at some meeting there. He was so tactless these days. The day he left, when she again asked him, tactfully, whether Kolya hadn't got into bad company there at Sverdlovsk, he had flushed scarlet and, with his back against the wall, shouted at her: "Do you realize what you're saying, or don't you? Kolya's not guilty of anything, what's the matter with you—don't you believe it?"

Of course he was not guilty of anything, there could be no question of it, but hadn't he perhaps given some cause for offence? . . . And now Alik, no doubt, had said something insolent to the authorities at a meeting. Naturally he must stick up for Kolya—but he must be cautious, tactful and restrained about it.

Olga Petrovna's head was aching. She felt as if the meeting were still going on. The voice of Timofeev was ringing in her ears. She felt she couldn't breathe—as though Timofeev's voice were constricting her. Should she lie down? No, that wouldn't do any good. She decided to take a bath.

There had been something about Timofeev's words that made her stiff with fear; perhaps if she took a bath, the feeling would pass. She went and got the wood from the cubby-hole herself and heated the geyser. Kolya used always to fetch the wood for her, then Alik fetched it; and after Alik had gone back to Sverdlovsk for the second time —Natasha!

What could you do with Alik! Of course he was a good boy, and devoted to Kolya, but he was so impetuous. It was no use blurting things out like that. Wasn't it perhaps because of something he'd said that Kolya had been picked up? In the queue once, on Shpalernaya Street, when she told Alik that they'd again refused to take the money for Kolya, he had burst out aloud: "Damned bureaucrats!" He might well have done something similar at the works in Sverdlovsk.

Olga Petrovna ran the water, undressed and got into the bath—the large, white bath, bought while Fyodor Ivanovich was still alive. She didn't feel like washing, but lay there, with her eyes closed. What was it going to be like at the office now without Natasha? And that Zoya Viktorovna there! To think that there were such envious, malicious creatures in the world! Never mind, Natasha would find herself another job, somewhere not far away, and they would often see each other . . . If only Kolya would return home soon! . . .

She looked at her arms, blurred by the water. Could it be that the secretary of the director was a wrecker? Better not to think about it. What a ghastly day it had been! The memory of the meeting still made her feel faint. She lay there with her eyes closed, in the peace and warmth.

In the kitchen, someone put out the primus, and she heard the sound of voices and the clatter of dishes. The nurse was, as usual, being spiteful. "I'm neither mad nor blind; I myself have bought three litres of oil a few days ago. And there's only a drop left on the bottom—might as well stuff it up you know where! Its become impossible lately to leave anything in the kitchen."

"Who's going to pinch your oil?" came the low voice of the militia-man's wife. You could hear that she was bending down, washing the floor, perhaps, or stoking the stove. "We've all got enough oil of our own. Me, do you think?"

"It's not you I'm talking about. There are others but you living in the flat. If one member of the family's in prison—the rest are capable of anything. It's not for nothing you get put in prison."

Olga Petrovna's heart stopped beating.

"What if the son *is* in prison," retorted the militia-man's wife. "Alright, he'll stay for a bit, and then they'll let him out. He's not a pick-pocket, or a common thief. A well-educated young man. All sorts of people get put in prison these days. My husband says lots of decent people are now being locked up. But this boy they even wrote about in the papers. A famous shock worker."

"Shock worker my foot! Just masquerading," came Valya's voice.

"I suppose you think he's just an innocent little lamb!" —the nurse was determined not to let the subject drop— "Excuse me, but people in our country don't get locked up for nothing. Chuck it! Take me, they haven't locked me up, have they? And why? Because I'm an honest woman, a real Soviet citizen . . ."

Olga Petrovna was seized by nervous shivering. Shaking as though in a fever, she dried herself, threw on her dressing gown, and tiptoed back into her room. She lay down under the blanket, and put a pillow on her feet. But still she couldn't get warm. She lay there trembling all over, and stared into the darkness.

About two o'clock at night, when everyone else was asleep, she got up, put on her coat, and went out into the kitchen. She collected her oil-can, her primus and her saucepans, and took them all back with her to her room.

It was morning before she fell asleep at last.

12

The next day, Olga Petrovna found Alik waiting for her outside the publishing house. Without saying anything to her beforehand, so as not to upset her for nothing, he and Natasha had queued up outside the prosecutor's office from early morning. Taking it in turns, they had queued for six hours, and the young lady at the hatch had told them, half an hour ago, that the case of Nikolai Lipatov was in the hands of the prosecutor Tsvetkov. They had then taken a place for Olga Petrovna in the queue for the prosecutor Tsvetkov. Office No. 7.

Alik tried to persuade Olga Petrovna to go home and have something to eat, but she was afraid to lose her place in the queue and set off as fast as she could go. She was going to save Kolya: his fate depended on what she was about to say to the prosecutor. She hurried on, gasping for breath, rehearsing her speech as she went. She would tell the prosecutor how Kolya, as a boy, had joined the Komsomol almost against his mother's wishes; how hard he had worked at school and at the institute, what a good reputation he had at the works, how he had been praised in *Pravda*, the central organ of the Party. That he was a fine engineer, a loyal member of the Komsomol, a devoted son. How could a person like that possibly be suspected of being a wrecker or counter-revolutionary? What absurd nonsense! She, his old mother, had come to testify to the judges that it was not true.

Alik pushed open the heavy door, and she went in.

Olga Petrovna had seen a lot of queues in the past few months, but never one like this. There were people standing, sitting and lying on every step, every landing and every window-sill of the vast staircase, going up five storeys. It was impossible to mount it without treading on someone's hand or foot.

The corridor round the hatch and leading to room No. 7 was jammed tight with people, like a tram. Those were the lucky ones, who had already queued all up the staircase. Natasha was standing hunched against the wall, under a poster proclaiming: "Up with the banner of revolutionary legality!" Having made their way to Natasha both took a deep breath. Alik took off his glasses and began to wipe them with his fingers.

"I'll go now," Natasha suddenly announced, "you're behind this lady".

Olga Petrovna wanted to tell Natasha about yesterday's meeting, and how she had spoken up in her defence, but Natasha was already gone, disappearing in the distance, near the stairs.

"Natalya Sergeevna's in a real mess," Alik said, "she can't get work anywhere. Like me."

He knew that Natasha had already applied to various places where they wanted typists but that when enquiries had been made at her previous place of work she had been turned down everywhere. Alik also, straight from the station, had applied to an engineering office—but when they heard that he'd been expelled from the Komsomol, they wouldn't even interview him.

"We've been put on the black list, obviously. Scoundrels! How is it there are suddenly so many dirty swine around?" Alik burst out in a rage.

"Alik!", exclaimed Olga Petrovna reprovingly. "How

can you talk like that? It was for using words like that that you were expelled from the Komsomol."

"It wasn't that, Olga Petrovna," protested Alik, his lips trembling, he was so hurt, "it was because I refused to disown Nikolai."

"No, no, Alik," Olga Petrovna protested gently, putting her hand on his sleeve. "You're still very young. I assure you, you're wrong. It's all a matter of being tactful. I, for instance, at the meeting yesterday, stood up for Natalya Sergeevna. And you see? Nothing happened to me. I tell you, this business with Kolya is a nightmare to me. I'm his mother. But I realize it's a temporary misunderstanding, due to exaggeration, muddle . . . you have to be patient. Instead of which you begin at once: scoundrels! swine! Remember what Kolya always said—there's an awful lot still wrong here, an awful lot of red tape."

Alik said nothing. His face wore a stubborn, obstinate expression; he was unshaven and pinched-looking, and there were dark marks under his eyes. And there was a fixed sullen look in his eyes.

"I have already sent a petition to the district committee. If they don't reinstate me, then I shall go to Moscow. Straight to the Central Committee of the Komsomol," he declared.

"Poor lad!" thought Olga Petrovna. "He's going to have a hard time while he's out of work. His aunt is probably already reproaching him." And Olga Petrovna bending towards Alik, whispered:

"You see, they'll release Kolya—and then you'll be reinstated at once." And smiled at him.

But Alik did not smile back.

The door of the prosecutor's office was still a long way off. Olga Petrovna counted forty people. They went in two at a time—there were two prosecutors interviewing people in room No. 7, not one—but even so, the queue moved very slowly.

Olga Petrovna examined the faces round her: she had the impression that she had seen most of those women before—on the Shpalernaya, or Chaikovsky Street, or here at the prosecutor's office; maybe they were the same, or perhaps they were different ones. All the women standing in the queues outside the prison had something similar about them: they looked tired, resigned, somehow secretive. Many of them were holding white slips—Olga Petrovna knew they were deportation "vouchers". Here in the queue three questions were heard all the time: "Where are you going?", or "When are you off?", or "Have you had your things confiscated?"

Olga Petrovna leaned against the wall and closed her eyes for a moment. What a heartless, malicious, stupid woman that book-keeper's wife was! Fancy imagining that Kolya was a wrecker! Why, she'd known him since a child! Olga Petrovna would never, never set foot in the kitchen again. Until that woman begged her forgiveness. Just imagine how ashamed she'd be when Kolya returned! Olga Petrovna would tell Kolya everything—about what marvellous friends Natasha and Alik were (but for them she simply couldn't have coped with the queues), and about that viper, the nurse. Let him realize what harpies there were in the world!

When she opened her eyes, Olga Petrovna noticed a little girl, who was crouching down against the wall. She was wearing a coat, buttoned all the way up to the neck. "How people muffle children up nowadays," thought Olga Petrovna, "even in summer." Then suddenly, she recognized the little girl: it was the daughter of the director,

Zakharov. The child was fidgeting about by the wall, snivelling and whining from the heat. And the tall, slim woman in the light suit—the one Olga Petrovna and Alik had been standing behind for the past hour—must be the director's wife. Yes, of course it was.

"How's your trumpet, not broken yet?" Olga asked with a smile, bending down over the child. "You've torn the tassel off, I expect? Do you remember me? At the New Year tree? Come here, let me unbutton your collar for you."

The child said nothing, looking at Olga Petrovna with big, round eyes, and hanging on to her mother's hand.

"What's the matter? Answer the lady!" the director's wife urged the child.

"I knew your husband," Olga Petrovna turned to her. "I work in the publishing house."

"Ah!" muttered the director's wife, a wry expression on her lips. She wore lipstick, but not on the lips, but above and below. A beautiful woman, no doubt about that—but Olga Petrovna no longer found her looking as young and elegant as she had been six months before, when she used to call in at the office to see her husband and bowed graciously to all the staff.

"What's happened about your husband?" enquired Olga Petrovna.

"Ten years in a distant camp."

"Then he was guilty, all the same. I would never have believed it. Such a nice person," thought Olga Petrovna.

"And they're sending the two of us to Kazakhstan, to some village or other, whatever you call them there ... We're off tomorrow. I'll die of starvation there in six months without work."

She spoke in a loud, sharp voice, and everyone turned to look at her.

"And where's your husband been sent to?" asked Olga Petrovna, in order to change the subject.

"How on earth should I know? As if they told you where!"

"But then how will you . . . in ten years' time . . . when he's released . . . how will you find each other? You won't know where he is, and he—he won't know where you are."

"And do you imagine," asked the director's wife, "that any of them"—and she gestured at the crowd of women with the "travel vouchers"—"know where their husbands are? The husbands have already been taken away, or will be taken away tomorrow, or today, the wives too will be sent off to some hell-hole, and haven't the foggiest idea how they're going to find their husbands when the time comes. How should I know? No-one knows, and I don't either."

"You have to persist," replied Olga Petrovna quietly. "If they won't tell you here, you have to write to Moscow. Or else, what's going to happen? You are going to lose sight of one another completely."

The director's wife looked her up and down.

"Who is it? Your husband? Your son?" she asked, so viciously that Olga Petrovna drew back closer to Alik. "All right then, when they send your son away, just you be persistent, go and find out where he is."

"My son won't be deported," said Olga Petrovna apologetically. "You see, he's not guilty. He was arrested by mistake."

"Ha-ha-ha!!"—the director's wife burst out laughing, carefully enunciating the syllables. "Ha! ha! ha! By mistake!" And suddenly her eyes filled with tears. "Here, you know, everything's by mistake . . . Oh!, stand still, can't you!" she shouted at the child, bending down to her, in order to hide her tears.

There were now five people between Olga Petrovna and the door. Olga Petrovna rehearsed to herself what she was going to say to the prosecutor. She thought with condescending pity about the director's wife: "That's husbands for you! It's they who make the mess, and leave their wives to suffer for it. She's now going off to Kazakhstan, with the child, and all these queues, too—its enough to make anyone a nervous wreck!"

"Listen, I'll go in with you," proposed Alik, "as a colleague and friend. I shall tell the prosecutor that Nikolai is absolutely pure and honest, an indomitable bolshevik. I shall tell him about how our works adopted the use of the Fellow's cog-wheel cutter, which we owe to the inventiveness of Nikolai."

But Olga Petrovna did not want Alik to accompany her. She was afraid of his impetuosity: he'd say something insolent, and ruin everything. No, she would do better to go alone. She assured Alik that the prosecutor only received relatives.

At last her turn came. The director's wife opened the door and entered. Olga Petrovna, with sinking heart, followed her in.

Near the wall, on either side of the dark, empty room, were two tables, each with a tattered armchair in front of it. Behind the table on the right sat a plump, white-faced man with china-blue eyes. Behind the one on the left, a hunchback. The director's wife and little girl went up to the white-faced man, Olga Petrovna, to the hunchback. She had heard tell in the queues, long since, that the prosecutor Tsvetkov was a hunchback.

Tsvetkov was speaking on the telephone. Olga Petrovna sank down into the chair.

The prosecutor Tsvetkov was short and thin, and

dressed in a greasy navy-blue suit. He had a sharp little head and a large, round hump. On his long wrists and the backs of his fingers was a growth of black hair. The way he was holding the telephone was not human but somehow ape-like. Altogether, Olga Petrovna thought he looked so much like an ape that she found herself thinking: "If he wanted to scratch behind his ear—he'd no doubt use his foot."

"Dubinin?" shouted Tsvetkov hoarsely into the telephone. "Tsvetkov here. How are you? Tell Rudnev, I've already checked everything. Let him send it. What's that? I said—let him send it."

At the other table, the plump, white-faced man with the blue, doll-like eyes and the small, plump feminine hands was talking politely to the director's wife.

"I want you to change me over from a village to a town of some sort," she was saying in a jerky voice, standing in front of the table holding the little girl by the hand. "In a village, I shall have no work. I shall have nothing to feed my mother and my child on. I am a shorthand typist. In a village there's no shorthand typing to be done. I ask you please to send me not to a village, but to some town—even a town in that—what do you call it?—Kazakhstan."

"Kindly take a seat, citizeness," the white-faced man invited her politely.

"What do you want?", Tsvetkov asked Olga Petrovna, putting down the receiver and giving her a glance with his little black eyes.

"It's about my son. His name's Lipatov. He was arrested owing to a misunderstanding, by mistake. I was told you were dealing with his case."

"Lipatov?", repeated Tsvetkov, pausing to recollect. "Ten years in a distant camp." And he took up the receiver again. "Section A? 244-16."

"What? He's already been tried?", exclaimed Olga Petrovna.

"244-16? I want Morozova."

Olga Petrovna sat there in silence, her hand on her heart. She felt her heart thumping slowly, throbbing in her temples and her ears. She decided to wait until Tsvetkov had finished, at last, speaking on the telephone. She looked in terror at his long, hairy wrists, his hump covered with dandruff, his unshaven, yellow face. Patience, patience! And again she felt her heart throbbing, in her temples and her ears.

At the table opposite, the white-faced prosecutor was speaking softly to the director's wife.

"There's no need for you to get upset, citizeness. Please take a seat. It is my duty, as the representative of legality, to remind you that the great Stalin constitution guarantees everyone, without distinction, the right to work. Since no-one has deprived you of any civil rights—you continue to enjoy the right to work, wherever you may be."

The director's wife stood up quickly and went towards the door. The little girl toddled unsteadily after her.

"You still here? What do you want?", snapped Tsvetkov, at last putting down the receiver.

"I would like to know, what my son was guilty of," replied Olga Petrovna, making a supreme effort to prevent her voice from trembling. "He has always been an irreproachable Komsomol, and a loyal citizen."

"Your son has confessed to his crimes. The investigation is in possession of his signature. He was a terrorist and took part in terrorist activities. Understand?"

Tsvetkov sat there opening and shutting drawers of the writing table. Pulling them out and banging them shut. The drawers were empty.

Olga Petrovna tried desperately to remember: what else was it she wanted to say? But everything had gone out of her mind. In that room, and with a person like that, anyway, no words were of any avail. She got up and made her way to the door.

"How can I find out now where he is?", she asked when she reached the door.

"That's not my business."

In the corridor, Alik was waiting for her. Silently they squeezed their way through the crowd in the corridor, and down the stairs. Silently they went out into the street, into the sunlight, with the rattle of the trams and the jostling of the passers-by. It was a hot, stuffy summer day, and evening was still a long way off.

"Well, what's happened, Olga Petrovna?" asked Alik anxiously.

"Sentenced. To a distant camp. Ten years."

"You can't be serious!" gasped Alik. "Whatever for?"

"Taking part in terrorist activities."

"Kolya—in terrorist activities? Raving nonsense!"

"The prosecutor says, he himself confessed. The investigation is in possession of his signature."

Tears were pouring down Olga Petrovna's cheeks. She stopped and clutched at the wall for support.

"Kolya Lipatov—a terrorist!" Alik was choking with indignation. "What swine they are, what utter swine! Why, it's fantastic rubbish! You know what, Olga Petrovna, I'm beginning to think all this is some colossal plot. Wreckers have got hold of the NKVD—and are running the show. It's they themselves who are enemies of the people!"

"But Kolya confessed, Alik, he confessed, you understand, Alik, you understand . . ." sobbed Olga Petrovna.

Alik took Olga Petrovna firmly by the arm and led her

home. Outside the door of the flat, while she was searching in her bag for her key, he began again:

"Kolya had nothing to confess to, surely you can't doubt that, can you? It's all completely beyond me, completely. There's only one thing I'd like to do now: to talk to Comrade Stalin, face to face. Let him explain to me what he thinks about all this!"

13

Olga Petrovna lay awake all night without even closing her eyes. How many nights ago was it since Kolya's arrest? It seemed an eternity.

She knew it all by heart already: the summer sound of feet under the window, the shouts from the beer-house along the street, the rumble of trams in the distance—then a short silence, and darkness—and then again the pale light filtering into the room, and another day beginning, a day without Kolya.

Where was Kolya now? What was he sleeping on? What was he thinking about? Where was he, and with whom? Olga Petrovna never for a moment doubted his innocence: terrorist activity? Raving nonsense—as Alik said. He must have come up against an investigator who was over-zealous, made him lose his head. And Kolya wasn't able to justify himself, he was still very young, after all.

Towards morning, when it was beginning to get light again, Olga Petrovna at last remembered the word she had been trying to think of all night: alibi. She had read about it somewhere. He had simply been unable to produce an alibi.

During the first hours at the office she felt a little better somehow. The sun was shining and the dust was dancing in the sunbeams; and the typewriters were clattering busily; in the lunch-hour the typists all ran down into the street and came back sucking choc-ices—it was all so familiar . . . but Kolya had been condemned—to ten years! Now, in the light of day, it became clear what utter rubbish this all was!

She wouldn't see Kolya for ten years. But why? What hideous nonsense! It simply couldn't be. One fine day— very soon—things would return to normal again: Kolya would be at home, arguing again with Alik, as he used to, about cars and locomotives, drawing plans again—only now she would not let him go to Sverdlovsk, whatever happened. There were jobs to be had in Leningrad, too.

In the lunch-hour she went out into the corridor to stretch her legs; she was afraid she might fall asleep if she stayed sitting at her desk. In the corridor the staff were crowding in front of a new wall-newspaper: a large special issue with headings in red letters and the portraits of Lenin and Stalin one on either side of the title, written in large bright-red characters:

OUR ROAD

Olga Petrovna went up to the newspaper.

> "How was it possible that wreckers were permitted, for five whole years to engage in their filthy activities with impunity under the very nose of Soviet society"

she read. It was the leader, by Timofeev.

In the next column was the beginning of an article by the chairman of the mestkom. Anna Grigorievna made a caustic attack on Timofeev because his speech at the meeting had not contained sufficient self-criticism. If society had allowed wrecking activities to pass unnoticed, the person mainly to blame was comrade Timofeev, the former Party organizer. Especially since, as it now transpired, the Party organizer had received timely warning from below: warning had been given by comrade Medvedeva, who, with her proletarian flair, had long ago smelt out the director's secretary.

Olga Petrovna went on to look at the next column. And before she grasped the meaning of what she was reading, she suddenly came over faint. The article was about her, Olga Petrovna, and how she had spoken in defence of Natasha. The author, whose identity was concealed by the initial X, wrote:

The meeting was marked by one scandalous occurrence to which, in our opinion, insufficient attention has been drawn. Comrade Lipatova spoke, like a veritable counsel for the defence—and whom did she deem it necessary to defend? Frolenko, a colonel's daughter, who had dared to hurl a gross anti-Soviet jibe at our beloved Red Army of Workers and Peasants. It is known that comrade Lipatova constantly favoured Frolenko, procured her overtime work, went to the cinema with her, and so on. Is it permissible, at this time, when the publishing house is being urged to enlist all the efforts of loyal workers and of Party and non-Party bolsheviks in order to liquidate, with all possible speed, the consequences of the Kuzmin "management", the regime of Zakharov and Co.—is it permissible, at such a time, to retain such persons on the staff of our publishing house? Up with the banner of bolshevik vigilance, in accordance with the teachings of our beloved leader, the genius of mankind, comrade Stalin! Let us root out all wreckers, both secret and open, together with those in sympathy with them!

X.

The bell rang for the end of the lunch-hour. Olga Petrovna went back to her office. How was it she hadn't noticed before that everyone was looking at her in a peculiar way today?

99

Back at home, she buried her head in her pillow—her last refuge. And fell asleep at once.

She slept a long time, and had a dream about Kolya. He was wearing a fluffy grey sweater. There were skates fixed on to his boots. And then, bending low, he was skating along the corridor of the publishing house.

When she woke up, dusk was already falling outside, but the light was on in her room. Natasha was sitting at the table, sewing. It was obvious she had already been there a long time.

"Come and sit here, nearer me," said Olga Petrovna, in a faint voice, passing her tongue over her lips, parched from sleep.

Natasha quietly brought over her chair, and sat down near the head of the bed.

"You know Kolya's been sentenced to ten years. Alik no doubt told you."

Natasha nodded.

"And you know?", Olga Petrovna said, remembering, "they wrote about me in the wall newspaper, saying that I had defended the wreckers, and that there was no room for me in the publishing house."

Natasha raised her head slowly:

"Alik has been arrested. . . . Last night . . ."

14

If Olga Petrovna didn't sleep at night, it made no difference to her what time of day or night it was. The light hurt her eyes, her legs ached and there was a gnawing feeling round her heart. But when she did manage to sleep at night, the worst moment, without any doubt, was just after she woke up. When she opened her eyes and caught sight of the window, the bottom of the bed, her dress hanging over the chair—for a moment she thought of nothing but these objects. But the next moment—she was seized by a feeling of dread, like a pain, starting somewhere in the region of the heart and, through the haze of that pain, everything suddenly came back to her: Kolya had been condemned to ten years, Natasha had been dismissed, Alik arrested, and about her they had written that she was hand in glove with the wreckers. Yes, and also—the oil.

At the office she no longer spoke to anyone. Even the papers brought to her for typing she handed to the typists without a word. And no one spoke to her either. From behind her desk in the office, she scrutinized the faces of the typists, trying to guess, who had written about her in the paper? Most likely—Zoya Viktorovna. Only she was surely not capable of writing so fluently. And when could she have seen her and Natasha at the cinema together? They hadn't once caught sight of her.

Loitering wretchedly in the corridor one day, she nearly ran into Natasha, looking like a sleep-walker, and picking her way carefully as though it were dark.

"Natasha, you here!", cried Olga Petrovna in surprise.

"I've been reading the paper. Don't speak to me. They'll see us!", whispered Natasha quickly.

That evening she came to see Olga Petrovna. She seemed to be in an excited state of mind and talked incessantly, jumping from one subject to another. Olga Petrovna had never heard Natasha talk so much. And for once she had brought neither embroidery nor sewing to do.

"What do you think, is Kolya still here in Leningrad, or far away already?", she asked suddenly.

"I don't know, Natasha," Olga Petrovna replied with a sigh. "On Shpalernaya Street it's the 20th for letter L, and today it's only the 10th."

"No, I don't mean that. What feeling have you about it?" Natasha made a gesture in the air. "Is he still here, near us, or a long way off already? I think he's a long way off. I suddenly had a feeling yesterday: he's far away already, I felt. He's no longer here. You know, Olga Petrovna, the lift-woman refused to take me up in the lift. 'I'm not obliged to take up people like you . . .' Olga Petrovna, you simply must get out of the office at once. Promise me you'll leave tomorrow. Please, my dear! Tomorrow—do you promise?"

Natasha knelt on the bed where Olga Petrovna was sitting, her hands clasped in entreaty.

Then she sat down at the table, seized a pen and herself composed a letter of resignation for Olga Petrovna. She assured Olga Petrovna that it was absolutely essential for her to resign voluntarily—otherwise she'd most certainly be dismissed for associating with wreckers, "that's with me", Natasha's pale lips smiled—and then no-one would take her on anywhere.

Olga Petrovna signed the letter of resignation. She'd

already thought of leaving herself. Things had become terrifying, somehow, at the office. The very sight of Timofeev limping along with the bunch of keys in his hand sent cold shivers down her back.

"In any case I shan't be able to work in Leningrad," she said sadly. "I shall be sent away, anyhow. All wives and mothers get sent away."

"What do you think?", asked Natasha, taking a book off the shelf and then putting it back again immediately, "why did Kolya confess? Of course a person can be tripped up, made to lose his head, that I understand—but only in small things. But how can Kolya have been reduced to such a state that he confessed to a crime which he never committed? That I simply cannot understand. And why do they all confess? All the wives are told that their husbands have confessed. They've all been made to lose their heads."

"He simply wasn't able to establish his alibi," explained Olga Petrovna. "You mustn't forget, Natasha, he's still very young."

"And why has Alik been arrested?"

"Oh, Natasha, if only you knew what awful things he's been saying in front of everyone in the queues. I am convinced it was his tongue that was the undoing of Kolya, too."

Natasha got up to go. As she said goodbye, she suddenly threw her arms round Olga Petrovna.

"What's the matter with you today?", Olga Petrovna asked her, in surprise.

"Nothing . . . Don't get up, please don't. How like Kolya you look, or rather, how like you Kolya is . . . You'll hand in your letter of resignation tomorrow, won't you? You won't change your mind?", she asked, looking Olga Petrovna straight in the eye. "And then don't forget, the 30th is the letter 'F', some money simply must be handed in for Alik, he hadn't a farthing on him, and his aunt will be too scared to take any along . . . And another thing, my dear, I beseech you, do please go and see a doctor. I beg of you! You're looking like death!"

"What's the use of a doctor . . . its Kolya! . . ." muttered Olga Petrovna miserably, her eyes full of tears.

Next morning, she went straight to the director's office and silently laid her letter of resignation on the glass-topped table. Timofeev read it through and nodded, also without a word.

All the formalities were completed with remarkable speed. Two hours later the announcement of her resignation was already posted up on the wall. Three hours later, the polite accountant handed Olga Petrovna her final pay packet.

"So you're leaving us, eh? That's bad. Mind you call to see us, you mustn't forget your old friends."

For the last time, she went along the corridor.

"Goodbye," she said to the typists, when the bell had gone and they were already banging down the lids on their Underwoods.

"All the best!" they all called out in answer, as they had done to Natasha not long ago; but one of them even came up and shook Olga Petrovna by the hand. Olga Petrovna was very touched: what a courageous, noble girl that was!

"Good luck!" sang out Zoya Viktorovna gaily, and suddenly the suspicion that had been tormenting her became an absolute certainty—it was Zoya Viktorovna who had written the letter, she and no-one else!

She went out into the street, into the din of the summer day. The sun was scorching down. No more going to the office—that was finished for ever.

She had meant to go home, but then decided to call on

Natasha instead. On all the street corners were small boys holding out bunches of bluebells and daisies in their sticky hands. Everything was just as usual, children even selling flowers. But because Kolya was in prison or being taken off somewhere to the rumble of wheels—the whole world appeared senseless and incomprehensible.

Climbing slowly up to the fifth floor—heavens, she was finding it more and more difficult to climb stairs!—she rang the bell. The door was opened by Natasha's neighbour, she was wearing an apron, and drying her hands on it as she spoke.

"Natalya Sergeevna was taken to hospital this morning," she said in a loud whisper. "Poisoned herself. With veronal. Mechnikov hospital."

Olga Petrovna stepped back. The woman slammed the door.

Number 17 tram was a long time coming. Two number 9's passed, and two 22's, but still no sign of the 17 . . . but there it came at last, stopped, and then trundled slowly on again, wearily, stopping at every traffic-light. Olga Petrovna stood. All the seats reserved for people with children were taken, and when the ninth woman with a baby got on, no-one was willing to give up his seat to her.

"They'll soon be filling up the whole tram!" cried an old woman with a stick. "Up and down they go, up and down! We in our time used to carry our children in our arms. Just you hold it, it won't kill you."

Olga Petrovna's knees were shaking, from fright, from the heat, from the old woman's vicious words. At last she got off the tram. She was certain, for some reason, that Natasha was already dead.

The hospital came into view, with all its shining clean windows. She entered the cool vestibule.

In front of the enquiries office was a queue—three people. Olga Petrovna did not dare go straight to the front, but waited her turn. Enquiries were answered by a pretty sister in a starched white overall. Near her, in front of the telephone, was a bunch of bluebells in a glass.

"Hallo, hallo!" she took up the telephone on hearing Olga Petrovna's enquiry. "Is that the second therapeutical ward?" Then, putting down the receiver, she said: "Natalya Sergeevna Frolenko died at four o'clock this afternoon, without regaining consciousness. Are you her relative? You may have a pass for admission to the mortuary."

15

On the evening of the nineteenth, Olga Petrovna put on her autumn coat with a scarf under it, and her galoshes, and went off to queue on the embankment. For the first time, she had to stand all night through. There was no-one to relieve her any more. Neither Natasha nor Alik.

Olga Petrovna had walked alone, right through the city, to the cemetery, behind Natasha's pinewood coffin. It was raining that day, and the great wheels of the horse-drawn hearse splashed the mud up into her face.

Natasha was lying in her grave, in the yellow earth, not far from Fyodor Ivanovich. But where were Alik and Kolya? It was impossible to understand.

She stood on the embankment the whole night through, leaning against the cold parapet. Cold damp rose from the Neva. For the first time in her life Olga Petrovna saw the sun rise here. It rose from somewhere beyond Okhta, and the surface of the river was suddenly rippled by tiny waves, as though it were being rubbed against the grain.

Towards morning, Olga Petrovna's legs went numb from fatigue, she had no feeling in them at all and when, at nine o'clock, the crowd rushed towards the door of the prison, she was incapable of running: her legs were like dead weights, and she felt as though she had to lift them up with her hands to make them move at all.

Her number this time was 53. Two hours later she reached the hatch, handed in the money and gave her name. The burly, sleepy-looking official looked at a card and then, instead of the usual "he's not allowed", answered "deported". Since the interview with Tsvetkov, Olga Petrovna had been fully prepared for this answer, but it stunned her nonetheless.

"Where to?" she asked, distractedly.

"He'll write to you himself . . . Next!"

She went home on foot—standing about waiting for a tram was more tiring than walking. It was hot and dusty, she unbuttoned her heavy coat and loosened her scarf. The passers-by seemed to have forgotten how to walk straight: they kept on knocking into her on all sides.

Kolya would write to her. She'd receive letters from him again, as she used to from Sverdlovsk.

Olga Petrovna now spent all her days looking for work, setting off early in the morning without getting breakfast or even making her bed. The papers were full of announcements: "Typists wanted." Her legs felt like lead, but she trudged round patiently all day, answering all the advertisements.

They asked the same question everywhere she went:

"Have you anyone who's been repressed?"

At first, she didn't understand.

"Relatives arrested," they explained.

She was afraid to lie.

"My son," she replied.

It then transpired that there were no vacancies on the staff.

And there was no vacancy anywhere for Olga Petrovna.

She was now afraid of everything and everyone. She was afraid of the watchman, whose indifference was, she felt, tinged with grimness. She was afraid of the house-manager, who no longer said good-day to her (she had ceased to be flat-representative, the book-keeper's wife had been elected to replace her). She was deadly afraid of the book-keeper's wife. She was afraid of Valya. She was afraid to go past the publishing house. Returning home after her fruitless search for a job, she was afraid lest she find a summons from the militia awaiting her. Perhaps they would summon her to the militia in order to take her passport away, and deport her? She was afraid of every ring at the bell: hadn't they come to seize her possessions?

She was afraid to go and hand over money for Alik. On the evening before the 30th, as she was on her way to join the queue, Nina Kiparisova came up to her. Nina Kiparisova mingled with the queue almost every day, and not on her day only, in order to find out from the women standing there what news there was: who had already been deported, who was still here, whether the timetable had been changed by any chance?

"You shouldn't be doing this," she whispered in Olga Petrovna's ear, when she told her what she'd come for. "Your son's case will be linked up with that of his friend— and things will look bad: Article 58, paragraph 11—counter-revolutionary organization. What's the good of that to you, I don't understand you!"

"But they don't ask the name of the person handing in the money," Olga Petrovna pointed out timidly, "they only ask who its for."

Nina Kiparisova took her by the arm and led her away from the queue.

"They don't need to ask," she said in a whisper. "They know everything."

Her huge, black eyes spoke of sleepless nights.

Olga Petrovna returned home.

The next day she didn't get up from her bed. There was

nothing to get up for. She had no desire to dress, put on her stockings or put her feet to the floor. What did it matter to her if the room was in a mess, what did she care about the dust?

She didn't even feel hungry. Just lay in bed thinking of nothing, not even reading. Novels had long since ceased to interest her: she was incapable of forgetting her own problems for a moment and concentrating on anyone else's. The papers filled her with vague terror: everything they wrote was like that article in the wall newspaper *Our Road* . . .

Now and again she pushed off the bedclothes and looked down at her legs: they were huge and swollen, and looked as if they'd been filled with water.

When the light on the wall faded and evening was approaching, she remembered about Natasha's farewell letter. It was still lying under her pillow. She must read it again. Propping herself up on her elbow, Olga Petrovna drew it out of the envelope:

"Dear Olga Petrovna!" Natasha wrote. "You mustn't weep for me, no-one needs me, anyway. For me it's better like this. Maybe everything will turn out all right, and Kolya will come home, but I haven't the strength to wait for that. I can't make sense of the present phase of the Soviet regime. But you must go on living, my dear one, the time will come when it will be possible to send him parcels, and he will need you. Send him tins of crab, he used to like it. Thank you for everything and for what you said about me at the meeting. I am sorry about what you have suffered because of me. You will have my tablecloth to remind you always of me. How we used to go to the cinema together—you remember? When Kolya returns, put it on his table, the colours on it are bright and cheerful. Tell him, I never believed anything bad about him."

Olga Petrovna put the letter back under her pillow again. "Perhaps I should tear it up. She writes about the present phase of the Soviet regime. Suppose they find the letter? Then they'll connect Kolya's case with Natasha's ... Or perhaps I can keep it? ... Natasha's already dead, anyway."

16

Three months went by, and another three, and winter came. January—the anniversary of Kolya's arrest. In a few months it would be the anniversary of Alik's arrest and, immediately afterwards, the anniversary of Natasha's death.

On the anniversary of Natasha's death, Olga Petrovna would go and visit her grave. But on the anniversary of Kolya's arrest, there was nowhere for her to go. She didn't know where he was.

No letter came from Kolya. Olga Petrovna looked into the post-box five, ten times a day. There were sometimes newspapers for the book-keeper's wife or post-cards for Valya—from her numerous young men—but never any letter for Olga Petrovna.

For over a year now she had not known where he was, how he was. Had he died? Could she ever have imagined that a time would come when she wouldn't even know whether Kolya was dead or alive?

She was already working again. It was only Koltsov's article in *Pravda* that had saved her from dying of starvation. A few days after the publication of that article—a remarkable article about slanderers and opportunists harming honest Soviet citizens for nothing—Olga Petrovna was taken on to work at a library: not on the permanent staff, certainly only on a temporary basis. But still, they did take her. Her job was to write out cards for the catalogue, in a special script: four hours a day, a hundred and twenty roubles a month.

At her new place of work, Olga Petrovna not only talked to no-one; she didn't even say good-morning, or good-bye, when she went. Bending over the table piled high with books, wearing glasses, her short grey hair falling down over her eyes, she sat out her four hours. When they were over, she got up, arranged the cards in a pile, took her stick with the rubber end which always stood beside her chair, shut the cards up in the cupboard and slowly, without a glance at anyone, went away.

There was a whole pile of tins of crab already standing on the window-sill in Olga Petrovna's room, and grains of buckwheat crunching underfoot; but still Olga Petrovna went round the food shops every day after work buying up more and more provisions. She bought tins, boiled butter, dried apples, lard—there was plenty of all these things in the shops at the moment, but by the time Kolya's letter came they might well have disappeared overnight.

Early in the morning sometimes, even before going to work, Olga Petrovna went along Obvodny Canal to the old clothes market. After bargaining fiercely, she bought a cap with earflaps, and some woollen socks.

In the evenings, sitting in her unheated, slovenly room, she stitched together all sorts of little bags, out of old rags. They'd be needed when the time came to make up a parcel. Under the bed were piles of plywood boxes of all shapes and sizes.

She now ate practically nothing—only bread and tea. She wasn't hungry, and anyway, she had no money. She didn't heat her room more than once a week, in order to save: food for parcels cost a lot. For that reason, too, she always put on her summer coat and mittens, when she was at home; when she was really cold, she simply got into bed. There was no point in cleaning up her room—it was cold and miserable anyway—so Olga Petrovna gave up sweeping the floor, and only flicked the dust off Kolya's books, the radio and the cog-wheel.

Lying in bed, she would compose her next letter to Comrade Stalin. Since the time when Kolya was arrested, she had already written three letters to Comrade Stalin. In the first one, she had asked him to review Kolya's case and have him released, since he was not guilty of anything. In the second, she had asked to be informed where he was, so that she might go there and see him once more before she died. In the third, she implored him to tell her only one thing only: was he alive or dead? But there was no answer. . . . The first letter she had simply dropped into the letter-box, the second one she had sent registered, the third one, with a return slip for confirmation of delivery. The return slip came back after a few days. In the column "Signature of recipient" was an incomprehensible scribble, in small letters: *eryan.*

Who was this mysterious *"eryan"*? And had he given her letter to Comrade Stalin? The envelope had been marked: *"Personal and private."*

Regularly, once every three months, Olga Petrovna went to one of the legal advice bureaus. She found the defence lawyers pleasant to talk to—they were polite, not like the prosecutors. There was a queue there too, but not much of one, only a matter of an hour or so. Olga Petrovna waited patiently, seated in the narrow corridor, resting her hands and her chin on her stick. But she waited in vain. All the lawyers, no matter whom she asked, told her there was, unfortunately, nothing to be done to help her son. Now if his case had been brought up for trial . . .

Then one day—it was one year one month and eleven days after Kolya's arrest—Nina Kiparisova appeared in

Olga Petrovna's room. She entered without knocking, gasping for breath, and sank down onto a chair. Olga Petrovna looked at her in amazement: Nina Kiparisova was afraid of Boris Ignatevich's case being linked up with Kolya's, and therefore never came to see Olga Petrovna. And now she had suddenly arrived, and was sitting there.

"They are being released," she said hoarsely, "people are being released. In the queue just now—I saw it with my own eyes—a man who'd been released came to fetch his papers. He wasn't thin, either, only his face was very white. We all crowded round him, asking: 'What was it like there?'—'It was all right,' he said."

Nina Kiparisova looked at Olga Petrovna. Olga Petrovna looked at Nina Kiparisova.

"Well, I must go now," Nina Kiparisova said, getting up. "I've got a place reserved for me in the queue for the prosecutor's office. Please don't see me off—we mustn't let anyone see us in the corridor together."

They were letting people out. Some people were being let out. They were coming out of the iron gates into the street, and returning home. Now they might release Kolya too. There'll be a ring at the bell—and Kolya will come in. Or no—there'll be a ring at the bell and the post-man will come in: a telegram from Kolya. Kolya's not here, but far away. He will send a telegram from somewhere on the way.

Olga Petrovna went out onto the landing and opened the door of the post-box. Empty, nothing inside. Olga Petrovna stood for a moment staring at the yellow side of the box— as though she could make it produce a letter.

She had only just got back to her room and was threading her needle (she was stitching up another bag), when some- one again opened the door without knocking, and the nurse appeared, followed by the house-manager.

Olga Petrovna stood up, her back to the stores of food, guarding them.

Neither the nurse nor the house-manager addressed a word to Olga Petrovna.

"You see!" the nurse rapped out, pointing to the oil-stove and the primus. "You just have a look: she's fixed up a veritable kitchen here. Soot, filth, she's blackened the whole ceiling with smoke. Destroying the communal pro-perty. She doesn't want to do her cooking in the kitchen, with the others—been sulking ever since we caught her out systematically stealing the oil. Her son's in a camp, exposed as an enemy of the people, she herself is without any fixed occupation, an unreliable element, in short."

"You, citizen Lipatova," said the house-manager, turning to Olga Petrovna, "take your cooking equipment out into the kitchen immediately. Or else, I'll report to the militia . . ."

They went out.

Olga Petrovna carried her primus, her oil-stove and her saucepans back into their old place in the kitchen; then lay down on her bed and burst out sobbing.

"I can't stand it any longer," she said aloud, "I just can't stand it any longer." And again, in a shrill voice, syllable by syllable, completely unrestrained: "I can-not, I can-not stand it an-y long-er . . ."

She pronounced the words as convincingly and per-sistently as if there had been someone standing there in front of her declaring that, on the contrary, she could easily stand more.

"No, I cannot stand it, it is impossible to stand it any longer!"

The militia-man's wife came into her room.

"You mustn't weep . . .", she whispered, wrapping Olga

Petrovna up in her blanket. "Just listen a moment to what I am saying. What they're doing is not legal. My husband says: since you've not been deported, no-one has any right to touch you. Don't you weep! My husband says a lot of people are being let out now—God willing, Nikolai Fyodorovich will return soon, too . . . That daughter of hers is off getting married soon—so her Mama's got her eye on your room. But don't you budge, that's all. Mama's trying to get hold of it for her daughter, and the house-manager's after it for his paramour. They'll come to blows over it . . . But just you don't cry! It's true what I'm telling you."

17

In winter, through the double windows, the sounds from the street scarcely penetrated into the room; but Olga Petrovna could hear the rustlings and creakings going on in the flat all night. First, the persistent gnawing of the mice —she only hoped they wouldn't get at the lard she'd bought for Kolya! Then in the corridor, the creaking of the floor-boards and, whenever a lorry went by, the rattling of the front door; and, in the book-keeper's room, a clock which struck solemnly every quarter of an hour.

Kolya would soon come back. That night, Olga Petrovna no longer doubted that Kolya would soon come back . . . Nina Kiparisova said so, and the militia-man, Doroshko . . . He must come back, because if he didn't she would die. If they were beginning to let out innocent people, then they'd soon let Kolya out too. It was impossible that they should release other people and not him. Kolya would come back—and how ashamed the nurse would be then. And the house-manager! And Valya! They wouldn't even dare to look at him. Kolya wouldn't even say good-day to them. He'd just look through them, as if they weren't there. When he came back, they'd give him a responsible job somewhere immediately—and even a medal!—in order to make amends for the wrong they'd done him. There'd be a medal on his chest, and he wouldn't even say good-day to the nurse or to Valya! . . .

Towards morning Olga Petrovna fell asleep, and it was ten o'clock before she woke up.

When she woke up, she remembered: something good had happened yesterday, she'd learned something good about Kolya. Ah yes! people were starting to be released from prison. And if they were being released, that meant that Kolya too would soon come back. And Alik. All would be well, as before. Olga Petrovna caught herself thinking: then Natasha, too, will come back.

No, Natasha would not come back.

But Kolya—why, Kolya was already on his way back, his train was perhaps already drawing into the station.

Returning from the library that afternoon, Olga Petrovna stopped in front of the window of a commission shop and stood for a long time gazing in. There was a Leica camera on show there. Kolya had long dreamed of possessing a camera. Suppose she sold something and bought Kolya the Leica to celebrate his return! Kolya would soon learn how to take photographs—he always picked everything up so quickly!

All that day Olga Petrovna felt happy and elated. She even felt hungry, for the first time in many days. She sat down at the kitchen table to peel some potatoes. Supposing she did buy Kolya a camera, there'd be the question of where he could develop his films. You needed a completely dark room. Ah! the cubby-hole, of course. There was wood there, but a place could be cleared. She could transfer part of her wood, little by little, into her own room, and ask the militia-man's wife to take a bundle into hers— she wouldn't refuse—that would make room. Kolya would photograph everyone: Olga Petrovna, the militia-man Doroshko and his wife, and their twins, and young ladies he knew—only Valya and her mother he wouldn't photograph on any account. He'd have a whole album full of photographs, but neither Valya nor her mother would ever get into his album.

"Have you a lot of wood left still in the cubby-hole?",
Olga Petrovna asked the militia-man's wife who had come
into the kitchen for her broom.

"About three bundles," she replied.

"Do you like having your photograph taken? I loved it,
when I was young, by a good photographer, of course . . .
You know what? Kolya's been released."

"You don't say!" exclaimed the militia-man's wife,
dropping her broom. "So you see! And you were making
yourself ill!" She kissed Olga Petrovna on both cheeks.
"What did he send, a letter or a telegram."

"A letter. I've only just got it . . . Registered."

"I didn't hear the postman come. You can't hear anything with these primuses going."

Olga Petrovna went back to her room and sat down on
the sofa. She felt she had to sit somewhere quietly, to
recover from her own words and grasp their meaning.
"Kolya's been released. They've released Kolya . . ." In
the mirror she saw a wrinkled old woman with dirty grey
hair streaked with white. Would Kolya recognize her, when
he returned? She stared into the mirror until everything
started swimming in front of her eyes, and she could no
longer make out which was the real sofa, and which the
reflection.

"You know, my son's been released. From prison," she
said to the woman who worked in the library with her, sitting at the same table writing out cards. Up till then, she'd
never heard Olga Petrovna utter a single word, and Olga
Petrovna didn't even know what her name was. But she felt
simply she had to repeat her statement, like an incantation.

"Well, now!" the woman answered.

She was a fat, untidy woman all covered with hairs and
cigarette ash.

"Your son, no doubt, wasn't guilty of anything—and so they released him. People in our country aren't kept in prison when they've done nothing . . . He was away for a long time, your son?"

"One year and two months."

"You see, they looked into the matter and then released him," said the fat woman, putting down her cigarette and turning back to her cards again.

That evening, the militia-man Doroshko, running into Olga Petrovna in the corridor, congratulated her.

"We'll have to celebrate!" he said, shaking her by the hand and smiling broadly. "And when will Nikolai Fyodorovich be coming to see his mother?"

"He'll put in a month or two at the works, then go to the Crimea for a rest—he needs a rest very badly—and after that he'll come and see me. Or maybe, I'll go and see him," replied Olga Petrovna, amazed herself at the ease with which she was saying all this.

She was happy and excited, she even walked faster. And she wanted to go round telling people all the time: "Kolya's been released. Did you know? They've released Kolya!" But there was nobody to tell.

That evening, going into a shop to buy bread, she ran into the polite accountant from the publishing house. Only the day before she had crossed over to the other side of the street when she saw him because everything reminding her of when she had worked there was painful. But now she smiled at him from afar.

He bowed gallantly, and asked at once:

"Have you heard our news? Timofeev's been arrested."

"What?", gasped Olga Petrovna. "But he—but it was he who exposed all the—all the wreckers . . ."

The accountant shrugged his shoulders.

"And now someone's exposed him . . ."

"You know, I've had good news," Olga Petrovna hastened to tell him. "My son's been released."

"Ah! Allow me to congratulate you. I didn't even know your son had been arrested."

"Yes, he was arrested, and now he's been released," said Olga Petrovna gaily, saying good-bye to the accountant.

Returning home, she looked automatically into the post-box. Empty. No letter. Her heart sank, as it always did at the sight of the empty box. Not a line for a whole year. Surely it must be possible to smuggle out a letter through someone? For a year and two months there had been absolutely no news of him at all. Could he be dead? Or was he still alive?

She lay down on the bed feeling that she'd never be able to get to sleep. But then she took some luminal, a double dose. And fell asleep.

18

"Today I received another letter," Olga Petrovna told them in the kitchen the next morning. "Just imagine, the director of the works has appointed my son to be his assistant. His right hand. The mestkom has procured him a travel voucher for the Crimea—there's gorgeous scenery there, I used to go in my youth. And when he comes back, he's getting married. To a Komsomol girl. Her name's Ludmilla—such a pretty name, isn't it? I am going to call her Milochka. She waited a whole year for him, although she had many other proposals. She never believed anything bad about Kolya." Olga Petrovna looked triumphantly at the nurse, standing beside her primus. "And now he's going to marry her—at once, directly he returns from the Crimea."

"Grandchildren! You'll be having grandchildren to fuss over!" The militia-man's wife's face was wreathed in smiles.

The nurse didn't so much as raise an eyebrow. But a moment later, when Olga Petrovna returned to the kitchen after going to her room to fetch some salt, she suddenly said "good morning" to her, as though she'd just seen her for the first time. The first "good morning" from her for a whole year.

It was Olga Petrovna's day off, and she decided to tidy out her room. Even if Kolya wasn't free yet, he was bound to be freed any moment now. He would arrive here—and everything in the room topsy-turvy!

Glancing at herself in the mirror, Olga Petrovna decided she simply must have her hair waved again. Nothing but dank, grey strands hanging down.

She pulled out some boxes from under the bed and lit the stove with them. The plywood burned easily, with a cheerful crackling. Olga Petrovna began to think: where could she store all those tins, cluttering the window-sill? And what did she need so many tins for? When she needed them she could always go to the shops and buy some.

She decided to wash the windows and the floor. Her legs were aching as they always did, and she had a pain in the small of her back, but never mind, you had to put up with that. She tore up the bags to use as rags.

While the water was heating, she must go and shake the carpet. Olga Petrovna dragged the carpet out onto the landing. Through the cracks of the post-box she could see there was something inside. Olga Petrovna, with an effort, went to fetch the key.

Inside the box was a letter. A rough, pink envelope. She read the inscription: "Olga Petrovna Lipatova." It was written in an unfamiliar hand. And there was no address on the envelope, no post-mark, nothing.

Forgetting all about the carpet on the landing, Olga Petrovna rushed back to her room. Sat down by the window and tore open the envelope. Who could it be from?

"Dearest mother!" it said, in Kolya's writing, and Olga Petrovna was so dazed by the sight of his writing that she dropped the letter onto her knee.

"Dearest mother! I am alive, and now a kind person has promised to take a letter to you. How are you, and where is Alik, and Natalya Sergeevna? I think of you all the time, my dear ones. It is terrible to think that you may now be living somewhere else, not at home. Mother, you are my only hope. My sentence was based on the evidence given by Pashka Gusev—you remember, a boy in my class? Pashka Gusev declared that he had persuaded me to join a terrorist organization. And I had to confess, too. But it is not true, there never was any such organization. Mother dear, the investigator Rudnev beat and kicked me, and now I'm deaf in one ear. I've written lots of appeals since I've been here, but have never had an answer. You must write yourself, saying you are my old mother, and put the facts before them. You know yourself that I never set eyes on Pashka Gusev after I left school, as he wasn't at the same institute as I was. And even at school I was never friends with him. They must have beaten him up badly, too. I embrace you fondly. Greetings to Alik and Natalya Sergeevna. Mother, you must do something quickly, I shall not last long here. Fond kisses, from your son

Kolya."

Olga Petrovna threw on her coat, jammed her hat down over her eyes and, still carrying a dirty rag in her hand, rushed off to see Nina Kiparisova. She was afraid she might have forgotten the number of her flat, and would not be able to find it. She clutched the letter in her pocket. She had left her stick behind, and ran along clutching at the walls. She felt her legs giving way under her: hurry as she might, she had still a long way to go before she came to the place where Nina Kiparisova lived.

At length she entered the building and, with a supreme effort, dragged herself up to the second floor. This must be it. Yes, this was it. "Kiparisova, N. V. Ring once."

The door was opened by a little girl, who immediately turned and ran away. Making her way past the cupboards in the dark corridor, Olga Petrovna pushed open a door at random, and went in.

Nina Kiparisova was sitting there in her coat on a trunk in the middle of the room holding a stick in her hands. The room was completely empty. Not a single chair, or table, not a bed or even any curtains—only a telephone on the floor near the window. Olga Petrovna sank down on the trunk beside the old woman.

"I am being deported," said Nina Kiparisova, showing no surprise at the sudden appearance of Olga Petrovna, and not even greeting her. "I'm off tomorrow morning. I've sold everything, and am going tomorrow. My husband has already been deported. For fifteen years. You see, I've already packed. There's no bed, nothing to sleep on, I'll sit up all night on the trunk."

Olga Petrovna handed her Kolya's letter.

Kiparisova sat reading it for a long time. Then she folded the letter up and slipped it into the pocket of Olga Petrovna's coat.

"Let's go into the bathroom" she whispered, "there's a telephone here. They've inserted some kind of special gadget into the telephone, and its become impossible to talk about anything—every word you say is heard at the exchange."

Nina Kiparisova led Olga Petrovna into the bathroom, put the hook on the door and sat down on the edge of the bath. Olga Petrovna sat down beside her.

"You've already written the appeal?"

"No."

"Then don't"! whispered Nina Kiparisova, bringing her huge eyes, ringed with yellow, close up to Olga Petrovna's face. "Don't write, for the sake of your son. They're not going to pat you on the back for writing an appeal like that, neither you nor him. And do you imagine you can write that the investigator beat him? You can't even think such a thing, let alone write it. They've forgotten to deport you, but if you write an appeal—they'll remember. And they'll push your son off farther away, too . . . Through whom was this letter sent, anyway? . . . And where are the witnesses? . . . What proofs are there?" She looked round the bath-room with distracted eyes. "No, for God's sake, don't write anything."

Olga Petrovna disengaged her hand, opened the door and went away.

In utter exhaustion, but still hurrying, she made her way home. She felt she had to lock herself in, to sit down and think things over. Should she go to the prosecutor, Tsvet-kov? No. To the defence lawyer? No.

She took the letter out of her pocket and threw it down on the table, then removed her coat and sat down by the window. It was growing dark and lights were already beginning to go on in the dusk outside. Spring was on the way, how late it got dark already.

She must decide, she must think it over. But Olga Petrovna simply sat by the window, thinking of nothing.

"Mother dear, the investigator Rudnev beat me . . ."

Kolya still wrote his "d's" with a loop. He always wrote them like that although, when he was small, Olga Petrovna had taught him he must write them with a downward stroke. She had taught him to write herself. On a lined exercise book.

It was now quite dark. Olga Petrovna got up to turn the light on, but simply couldn't find the switch.

Wherever was the switch in this room? She fumbled all along the wall, knocking into the furniture which she had moved out of place in order to clean the room.

She found it. And caught sight of the letter immediately. It was lying, creased and crumpled, on the table.

Olga Petrovna took a box of matches out of the drawer. She struck a match and set fire to the corner of the letter.

The letter burned. The corner curled slowly over, coiling up until it burned her fingers.

Olga Petrovna threw the flame down on the floor and stamped on it.

19 November 1939 – February 1940